ME, MYSELF and iKE

AR
4.2
5.0

ME, MYSELF and IKE

K.L. DENMAN

ORCA BOOK PUBLISHERS

Library and Archives Canada Cataloguing in Publication

Denman, K. L., 1957-
Me, myself and Ike / written by K.L. Denman.

ISBN 978-1-55469-086-2

1. Schizophrenia in adolescence--Juvenile fiction.

I. Title.

PS8607.E64M4 2009   jC813'.6   C2009-902805-0

First published in the United States, 2009

Library of Congress Control Number: 2009928211

Summary: Seventeen-year-old Kit is paranoid, confused and alone, but neither he nor his family and friends understand what is happening to him.

Orca Book Publishers gratefully acknowledges the support for its publishing programs provided by the following agencies: the Government of Canada through the Book Publishing Industry Development Program and the Canada Council for the Arts, and the Province of British Columbia through the BC Arts Council and the Book Publishing Tax Credit.

Design by Teresa Bubela
Cover artwork by Getty Images
Author photo by Hannah Denman

ORCA BOOK PUBLISHERS
PO Box 5626, STN. B
VICTORIA, BC CANADA
V8R 6S4

ORCA BOOK PUBLISHERS
PO Box 468
CUSTER, WA USA
98240-0468

www.orcabook.com
Printed and bound in Canada.
Printed on 100% PCW recycled paper

12 11 10 09 • 4 3 2 1

For the moon and the meadow, with love.

I am in you and you in me, mutual in divine love.
WILLIAM BLAKE

FIVE THOUSAND YEARS AGO...

The men are weary. The light is fading. By now they should have arrived at their destination and delivered the copper ax. It's clear they've gone astray, perhaps into enemy territory.

They make camp for the night, huddled in the lee of an overhanging rock. Their fire, which wards off both the mountain cold and the possibility of animal attack, is a calculated risk. Should hostile eyes happen to sweep over them, the smoke will betray their presence, but surely the blowing snow that has obscured the landmarks all day will conceal one small thread of rising smoke. Surely.

They eat quickly, sharing deer meat, flat bread and fruit, and then they notice that the rock above them, its silhouette stark against a star-strewn sky, resembles a fearsome beast. A bad omen. And yes, the treacherous snow has elected to depart, exposing their fire. They argue about dousing it, weigh again their conflicting needs. In the end, a small fire blazes on. Neither of them sleeps.

At first light they set out, plodding steadily on their snowshoes, heading for their home village. Delivery of the ax will have to wait. The stars have at least given them direction, the sun too in its rising. They keep their weapons in hand.

The attack, when it comes, is hardly a surprise. Their enemies are clumsy and overconfident as they attempt to encircle the pair. So noisy, so foolish. The travelers' first arrows find their marks. So do the next. Perhaps they will escape? Hope flares, hot as breath, as they forge on, eyes darting among the trees for a glimpse of further threat. Have they won? Is it possible?

It is not. The air parts, hissing, and they are hit, one in the shoulder and the other in the arm. They do not fall. They let fly swift replies and now...Now it is done. Incredible. The adrenaline rush of victory allows them to retrieve precious arrowheads, to nod admiration, one for the other. But when that rush has run its course, their wounds begin to speak of pain, of loss, of death.

No, not death. The one most sorely wounded still stands, and the other too. They lean together, share support and go on. How long they struggle forward, neither of them can say. Sweat runs from their brows, but it is as nothing compared to the running of blood.

They sink into the snow, and now they can see that the arrow to the arm was little more than a graze, a flesh wound, easily bound. But that one still lodged in the other's shoulder...It is not good.

"Hold steady now, and I will remove it. Lie down," says the one with the grazed arm.

The other lies down, bites hard on the flap of his bearskin hat. He does not cry out as the arrowhead grinds against bone, but a low groan escapes when he hears the shaft splinter free.

"The arrowhead refuses to leave you. It is deep. There is much blood."

The man on the ground nods. After a moment, he says, "You must go."

His companion shakes his head. "No."

"You must. No need for our tribe to lose two metal masters."

"I will get help. We will come back for you."

"It will be too late. Take the ax."

"No. It is a token of my word that I will return. I leave it with you for safekeeping; its weight would burden me."

"It is too valuable to leave behind. Take it."

But his companion does not.

The man on the ground reflects on his life. He doesn't believe he'll see his tribe again. He would like a proper burial, a ritual to secure his return. All of life returns, does it not? He feels his strength seeping away in steady throbs. He looks about and decides that this unfamiliar place will not do. He stands. Takes one step. Two. More. How many? It doesn't matter. He must find the proper resting place.

His gaze sweeps from side to side, and he sways, falls backward, feels only dimly the crunch of his skull on rock. Vision fades for a time but when it returns, so too does his compulsion, driving him upright once more. There is blood on the snow, and a shudder takes him; he must distance himself from that. He must. He staggers on, forcing step after step from his broken body, going until he can go no farther. His time has come. He looks about, salutes the holy earth, left hand to heart, and collapses, pitching forward. There is no more pain, no awareness of the avalanche that comes snarling to cover him in white so deep its marrow is black.

ONE

I pace the crumbling sidewalk in front of the old concrete building twice before I glance down the alley and see a sign jutting out. The faded slab of wood hangs crookedly, but the flaking paint says I've found what I'm looking for: *Tony's Tattoos*. I slip into the alley's dank shade and adjust the hood on my black sweatshirt, turtling into its depths as I push open the door.

I get a dim impression of clutter, stale cigarette smoke, ragged posters of tattoo designs papering the walls, but I don't look at these things. I focus on the guy huddled over the spotlighted flesh of a woman's bare thigh. He's wielding a tattoo gun with squinting concentration. He doesn't look up.

He says, "Yeah?"

The woman he's working on remains motionless, but her eyes probe mine and she mutters, "Jeez. Do you mind?"

I hadn't counted on there being any other customers in a crappy shop like this. I'd pictured myself walking in, demanding my tattoo, getting it and getting out, just like that. I look at the walls and say, "Maybe I'll come back later."

The guy, probably Tony, says, "Almost done here. What've ya got in mind, kid?"

Kid? I start to lie, tell him I'm no kid, I'm plenty old enough to do this, but he asked what I wanted, didn't he? Maybe he won't ask for ID.

"I've got my design right here." I pull a piece of paper out of my pocket.

Briefly, Tony's eyes squeeze shut. "Of course ya do. Doesn't everyone these days? Sure you don't want to take a look at my book? It's right there, on the counter. I do a nice serpent. Pretty nice skull too."

"No thanks."

For the first time, he looks up. He's still squinting when he asks, "Ya got cash? It's one twenty an hour."

I nod.

"Okay, take a seat. Be with you in a few."

"You're being careful, aren't you, Tony?" the woman whines. "You're not hurrying, are you?"

"Cupcake, I'm just like a granny on ice. Don't worry. It's gonna be amazing."

She allows herself a small smile, then winces as the needle moves close to the bone. "Good. This is for my latest guy, y'know."

"Yeah, yeah." Tony snorts. "Gotta tell ya, Penny, I hope he goes the same way as the last one."

"What?" she screeches.

He chuckles. "Relax. You and your guys—you're good for business."

"Tony!"

"All right, all right. I hope you live happily ever after."

I tune them out. I pick up the book of designs and slump into a ratty chair in the corner. I start flipping through but barely register the roses, the ships, the hula girls, all the old-school stuff. Only one stands out: a white stag with intricate antlers crowning his head. The eyes of the stag are uncanny, almost life-like. It makes me pause. White stags are such powerful symbols of…something.

My thoughts drift and settle on my conversation with Ike, the one that led to this. He had said, "The Ice Man had tattoos. You're going to need some."

I said, "Right. Like my folks are going to sign off on that one. Forget it."

"You're such a freakin' pussy, Kit," Ike said. "You try hard enough, you'll find someone who'll do it. Or you could do it yourself, though I doubt you'd have the balls for that."

"Do it myself? Get real."

"You think the Ice Man went to a tattoo parlor? Dudes have been doing their own tatts forever, man. Just like piercing. You don't need a pro for any of that shit. Bet you could go on the Net and find out how to do it in ten seconds."

I thought about it. But if I was going to get a tattoo, it would have to be hidden someplace where my parents wouldn't notice it. And if I was doing it to be like the Ice Man, then shouldn't it be on my lower back or behind my knee? How was I supposed to do that myself?

"So you take the bus to Nanaimo," Ike said, "or even Victoria. Probably lots of places there. You find a joint that isn't too bugged about rules and *bam!*— you're done. Look at how many kids at school got tatts. There's places that'll do it."

There aren't that many kids at my high school with tattoos, but there are a few. If they could figure it out, then I could too. And Ike was right; there were a few places to choose from in Nanaimo. I'd called them all, and I had a hunch Tony's was a good bet. His directory ad was tiny, he didn't have a website and when I spoke to him on the phone, he didn't ask any questions.

Tony interrupts me now. "Kid? Let's take a look at what you've got."

I stare at him for a moment, uncomprehending, and he holds out his hand. "Your design? You said you brought it?"

Wordlessly, I hand it over. He frowns as he studies it. "Just looks like a bunch of little lines and dots and a word. What's this say? Awtzee?"

"Close enough," I tell him. The word is *Ötzi*.

"What's that?" Tony asks.

"Not what. Who."

"Ha," he grunts. "Funny name for a girl." He looks over at Penny, who is pulling on a snug black jacket. "Hey, cupcake. We've got another romantic here."

Penny grins. "Good for you, kid. Hope she appreciates you."

I shrug. If they don't know who Ötzi is, I'm not going to tell them. Penny heads out the door, and Tony motions me toward his table. He flexes his hands and takes a long swallow from a water bottle. "So you know where you want this tattoo?"

"I want the name on my lower back. And the short parallel lines and dots on the back of my left calf. And some around my right ankle. All in black."

Tony's brows go up. "You sure about that? It's usually the girls who want the lower-back thing." He pauses and runs his glance over my skinny frame. "Well, could be Awtzee's a guy too, eh? None of my business."

My face burns. I know what he's thinking. I'm not gay, but it's not like it would matter if I was. Especially now. I muster a firm voice. "On the lower back."

Tony shrugs. "No problem. Just don't like to see anyone make a mistake and get a tattoo they end up hating."

"I'm not making a mistake."

"Okay then. You said you got cash, right? I figure this'll be max two hours. Depends on how many lines and dots you want."

"I've got enough for two hours. Maybe just do what you can until the time's up?"

He laughs. "Sure. Let's get started. Take off your shirt and lie face down on the table. The name in black ink too?"

I nod and take off my hoodie. I leave my T-shirt on and just scrunch it up under my armpits before I lie down and take a deep breath. I feel Tony's hands on my lower back, then the light touch of felt pen, and I try to feel the letters as he sketches. I have a sudden memory of me and my brother Fred tracing words with our fingers on each other's backs and trying to guess what we'd written.

"Old English-style lettering is okay with you, isn't it?" Tony asks.

"What do you mean?"

"The style of the letters. Old English is the usual."

I hadn't thought about letter styles so I just shrug.

"I wouldn't do that again if I were you, kid. You've gotta hold still."

"Sorry," I mutter.

"Okay, here we go," Tony says. And just like that, the needle is into my skin. I tense, and Tony says, "Relax. This is as bad as it gets."

It isn't so bad. More sting than pain. The tattoo machine buzzes, and I try to focus on that sound. It reminds me of something, and I'm trying to figure out what when Tony mutters, "Ötzi."

I wait for him to say more but he merely snorts, a sound that manages to dismiss me. I decide it's a good thing he's not curious about why I chose this tattoo, because I wouldn't want to explain. I focus again on the drone of his machine, but whatever it reminded me of has dodged away. I don't like it though. There's something threatening in that sound, like the buzz of wasps, and my muscles tighten.

"Gotta remember to relax, kid," Tony says. "We've barely got started."

Relax, he says. How am I supposed to do that? Now that I think about it, it's been a while since life seemed easy. Back when I was a kid, nothing was complicated. Like when I used to hang around with my best bud, Ben, and we'd do simple stuff like jump on his trampoline.

Yeah, that was good. We flew high on that tramp, didn't think about anything else when we were into that straight-up fun. Ben outweighed me by about twenty pounds, and sometimes his bounce sent me helter-skelter, way up into the sky. I loved that feeling of being airborne, that moment of suspension in space before gravity took me back to the quivering surface of the tramp. I'd splat down, and we'd laugh like maniacs.

We did fake WWE moves on each other too. Ben could take my scrawny twelve-year-old body down any time he wanted. Only he didn't. Ben wasn't like that, never felt like he had to prove anything to me. When we'd had enough, we'd lie back on the warm rubber, catch our breath and stare up at the sky.

"Someday," I told him, "I'll go up, and I won't come down for a long time."

"Yeah, right," Ben scoffed. "You going to be wearing your Superman cape for that?"

I laughed. "I was thinking about being a pilot, but if you know where I can get a cape, bring it on."

"A pilot? For real?"

"Yeah. It would be so cool." I did want to be a pilot. I'd look up at the sky and see a whole world of possibility opening out beyond the enclosed rectangle of the backyard. A plane could take me there.

I asked Ben, "What do you want to do?"

His shoulders moved uneasily. "No idea."

"None?"

"None. Zip. Zero. Nada."

I told him he could be my copilot.

"Yeah?" he said. "Well that might be cool. Are you serious, Kit? About being a pilot?"

"Why wouldn't I be? I could travel the world, see everything, be up there in the sky going faster than sound...It would be amazing."

But when I looked at Ben, he was looking the other way and his mouth was pulled sideways, his brow furrowed.

"What?" I asked.

"I doubt I could ever do something like that."

"Why not?"

"'Cause…I dunno. It just seems unreal, right? Like a fantasy. And I guess I sort of like knowing where I'm at." That was Ben; he liked to watch crime or reality shows on TV, never did go in for fantasy.

So I just told him, "You're right. It's good to know where you're at."

Ben didn't always know where he was at. I remember the first time I saw him, about five years ago. He was new in town, and he was alone in the park, orange hair and freckles making him a standout. A group of guys were there and they started to hassle him. It wasn't anything too serious, mostly just cracks about his hair, but even from a distance Ben's rigid posture told me he was looking for a way out.

I knew those guys a bit, knew they were more mouth than anything, but they could get ugly at times. I walked over, said "hey" to them and tossed Ben my basketball. "So, ready to shoot some hoops?" I said. Ben caught the ball, and his face broke into this big surprise-party grin of gratitude; we've been friends ever since.

"That's it, kid. All done."

I'm jolted back to the present, back to the dingy tattoo parlor and Tony saying, "Want to check out the new you in the mirror?"

Two

The bus ride home takes under two hours but it feels longer. I want to check my new tattoos, see if they're okay, and I wish Ike was with me to tell me if Tony did them right. A few weeks ago, Ike and I watched a documentary on TV. The program was about Ötzi, the guy who died on a mountain in Italy over five thousand years ago. His corpse was found by a couple of German tourists who were out hiking in the Ötztal Alps. He's the oldest natural mummy ever found in Europe.

The authorities hauled Ötzi's body out of his melting glacier, picked up his stuff and took him in for examination. At first they thought his body hadn't been there very long, but they quickly learned the truth. And then they went all out. They x-rayed and dissected and analyzed. They figured out all kinds of stuff, like what he'd eaten for his last couple of meals, what he might have done for a living (either a shepherd or a dude who smelted copper), how he might have died (blood loss from an arrow wound plus a blow to the head). They found fifty-nine carbon tattoos on his skin: simple dots and lines on his lower back, on his left leg, around his right ankle and around his left wrist.

The stuff Ötzi had with him included a copper ax with a yew handle, a flint knife, a longbow and a quiver of fourteen bone-tipped arrows. A couple of his arrowheads had traces of human blood on them. He was wearing a bearskin hat and clothes made out of woven grass and leather. He was carrying berries and a couple of birch-bark baskets. Me and Ike were gobsmacked.

I said, "Man, can you believe how much they can figure out from an old dead body and a few things he had with him?"

"Freakin' incredible," Ike said.

"It's the crazy science we've got now. DNA testing and stuff. That blood on his clothes? They even figured out there was another guy on the scene."

Ike laughed. "Yeah. *CSI: Alps.*"

"Absolutely. Forensics are cool. I mean, once you get past the part about being around dead bodies. If they'd found Ötzi even a hundred years ago, they wouldn't have been able to figure out half of this. Imagine what they'll be able to do in another five thousand years."

"You actually think people will survive another five thousand years?" Ike asked.

I shrugged. "Who knows?"

"If we do last that long, we'll be the ones who look prehistoric. We can shake our heads over the guy's mushrooms on a leather string and his cloak of grass, but if someone from the future saw our stuff, they'd probably start saying 'Ooga chucka.'"

"Ooga chucka?"

"You know. Caveman talk."

"No way. They'd be able to tell we're beyond that. Our artifacts would show them how advanced we are."

"Yeah? What artifacts are those?"

"Just think about it," I said. "What would a guy today be carrying around in a backpack?"

Ike said, "You tell me."

"Okay. He might have books. Maybe an iPod. Some food. A cell phone. Some extra clothes or sports gear."

"Sports gear would tell the future how smart we are?"

"No. But it would be part of the picture. It would show them we liked to have fun."

Ike laughed. "Fun? You know what would really be fun?"

"What?"

"Being an Ice Man. Present day."

"What do you mean?" I asked.

"Just what I said. You gather up some modern stuff, which, five thousand years from now, will be ancient stuff, and you stash it on a mountain, along with a body. The body itself becomes another artifact."

"That's sick, man. Are you talking about getting a dead guy and taking him up a mountain?"

"No. Duh. I'm talking about you being the next Ötzi. You'd be famous."

"Uh, yeah. But I'd also be dead."

"So? All famous people end up dead. Most of the ones who are famous today won't mean squat a hundred years from now. All these actors and rock stars—who's going to even know their names? But a guy who's, like, a messenger from the past, that's special. Extraordinary. You should do it."

"Why me?"

Ike heaved a sigh. "Why not you? What have you got going on in your miserable little life anyhow? You don't have any friends, except for me. You don't do anything. You suck at school. You've got no idea what you want to do after you graduate this June. You're a nobody. This is your chance to be a some-body, Kit." He snickered. "A some *body*. Get it?"

I got it. He was right. My life was crap and getting worse all the time. Still. He was talking about dying, and I wasn't sure I wanted that either.

He went on. "Freezing to death is supposed to be a good way to go. Just like falling asleep and never waking up. Real calm. Real quiet. And you like the mountains, don't you?"

"Yeah." I do like the mountains. And that part about quiet and calm? I'd like that too. "What about you?" I asked.

"Hey, man, if you do it, I just might do it too. I'll help you figure it out anyway."

I was quiet, imagining this death on a mountain. Was he right that it was painless? I doubted that. "Freezing has to hurt. Before you fall asleep. Your survival instincts would kick in and you'd fight it."

"Yeah, maybe. But here's what you do. You take along a nice bottle of whiskey." He chortled, then added,

"Like that kind they serve in the Yukon, whatchama-callit, Yukon Sourtoe."

"What's that?"

"It'd be perfect. It's where they put someone's frozen toe into your shot of whiskey, and when you drink up, you've gotta be sure the toe touches your lips."

"They put in an actual toe? A human toe?"

"You got it."

"Man, that's disgusting."

"Guess it is for weenies like you. So don't get the whiskey. Get a nice big two-six of vodka. You down it, pass out, and that's it. Game over."

"Where am I going to get a two-six of vodka?" I asked.

"Come off it. Fred might boot for you, right? Or check out your parents' liquor cabinet. Didn't they stock up for that Christmas party they had? Bet there's leftovers."

There were leftovers. Lots. I knew that. I told him I'd think about it. But Ike is like a pit bull: he gets hold of something and he doesn't let it go. Over the next few days, he convinced me. I would be the next Ice Man. I would be somebody.

Somebody.

That reminds me of another time I was watching TV, a few years ago, with my family. We started off watching a documentary that time too, about World War II. I remember I didn't like it, all the footage of soldiers in tanks, in bomber planes, marching in combat boots. Scenes flashed across the screen, images of emaciated bodies piling up in pits, images of children screaming, of an enormous mushroom cloud…

"I can't take this," Mom said. "Isn't there something else on, like a nature show?"

"This *is* nature," Dad said grimly. "Human nature."

I said, "It's disgusting."

"Yeah," Dad agreed, "it is. But it's a reality we shouldn't forget. We have to remember, otherwise we'll make the same mistakes again. We need to learn from the past."

I couldn't keep watching. I said I had to finish my homework. I went to my room, opened my books and tried solving some math problems. But behind the numbers, the grotesque images from the TV rose up and I felt nauseous. Helpless.

I gave up on the math and thought hard about how I'd run the world, given the chance. There wouldn't be such a thing as war in my world, no starvation, no pillaging of the planet. People would cooperate. They'd work together, get along, respect one another.

I thought harder yet about how to make this happen, how one of the first things I'd do is ban all weapons. It would be a large job because I figured people have been at war since there were people. How could they be convinced to put aside their differences? I didn't know. I ended up looking out the window. A bird flew past, and I remembered that I wanted to be a pilot. Not an army pilot though.

I called Ben and it took a while for him to pick up.

"Hey," Ben muttered.

"What's up?" I asked.

Ben paused. "Not much. Just playing *Civilization*."

Civilization was our favorite computer game. I paused too, as images of conquest and war resurfaced. Then I remembered that Ben was mad at me. I hadn't done anything, not on purpose anyway. It was that girl, Justine, who caused the problem. Ben liked her, and when he finally got up the courage to talk to her, all she wanted to talk about was me.

Back then, quite a few girls seemed to have a thing for me. I didn't know why, and one of my basketball buddies, Joel, said his sister told him a lot of the girls thought I was hot. Joel played it up, put a towel around his face, puckered his lips and mimicked his sister's voice: "Ohhh, Kit is soooo adorable. He's got those amazing blue eyes, and he moves like a dancer on the court. Plus he looks so sweet and mysterious and *sensitive*."

Man. We were in the locker room after a practice and all the guys cracked up, carrying it on for a while. I was embarrassed but flattered too, in an uneasy sort of way. I didn't know what to do with this information, just knew I'd never live up to the stud label some of the guys gave me. Ben thought it was funny too, up until Justine, but he had to know that wasn't my fault.

"So," I asked him, "are we okay?"

"Whatever," Ben muttered. "Yeah."

"Good. Later then?"

"Yeah. See ya tomorrow."

I went back downstairs, made popcorn and took the bowl into the family room to share.

My parents had switched to watching a stand-up comedy show. They were laughing at the jokes, and soon I was laughing too. I felt better. Everyone just needed to lighten up—that was the solution. The last comedian was the best, a guy who did a routine about his immigrant father, who laid on beatings, but only after giving a warning: "*Somebody's* gonna get hurt real bad."

The comedian said he always found hope in the word *somebody* because maybe, just maybe, it meant that he wasn't the one about to get hurt.

Three

I get home from the tattoo parlor around the same time I would have if I'd gone to school, and as usual no one else is there. There's a message from my school on our answering machine, reporting my absence. I delete it. I'm in my room, parked at my computer, by the time Mom gets home. Hard to believe how easy it all was.

She opens my door, pokes her head in and says, "Hi, Kit. Doing your homework?"

I nod.

At this point she should leave, but instead she walks in. I minimize the page on the screen and say, "What?"

She sighs. "Nothing, really. I was just thinking. You haven't been seeing much of your old friends lately." There's a pause and she adds, "Have you?"

She isn't sure. That's how much she knows about me. There was a time when she knew pretty much everything, back when she stayed home with me and Fred. But at some point I guess she got bored, figured we didn't need her so much anymore, and she returned to the work she did BC—her jokey little acronym for Before Children.

"I see them as much as ever," I say. "Guess you're just not around enough to keep track."

Again with the sigh. "If you say so, Kit. You're sure everything's all right?"

I give her a sideways look. "I'm fine, okay?"

She sets her hand on my shoulder. "Okay. I'm going to make dinner. Just remember, if you need to talk, your father and I are here for you."

"Yeah, right," I mutter. But when she flinches, I relent and add, "Thanks."

She gives my shoulder a parting pat and turns to go. I listen to her footsteps crossing my room, listen for the door closing behind her, keep listening as her steps carry her down the stairs and the sound fades. Part of me wants to follow her and tell her, Yes, Mom, something is wrong. But I wouldn't know what to say after that.

"What's wrong?" she'd ask. And I'd be stuck.

How can I tell her that it's not me, it's everyone else, including her, who isn't right? Not that she'd change anything if I told her to. Not that I want her to. No, I like the privacy, the quiet, the freedom. I need it. I'd go crazy if she was around all the time, watching me. Besides, she loves her paralegal job, likes wearing the nice clothes, hanging out with her coworkers. She really wouldn't want me to tell her there's a problem. She wants me to say I'm okay.

I maximize the web page and continue checking out the latest in Blackberries. The one I need costs plenty, but it's state-of-the-art. Of course it includes a phone and the standard Internet stuff, but it also has a built-in camera, video, MP3 player and GPS. How cool is that? I make a note of the model number, then move on to my music list.

The Blackberry can hold hundreds of songs, and that's good, but it's not easy to figure out which ones are necessary. I mean, I'm no expert on the latest, greatest in music and that's subjective anyway. The best tunes to one person might be the worst to another. I could just go with my own tastes, but I'm trying not to make this personal. It's got to be generic, which might turn out to be a jumble, but if I'm creating a musical time capsule—yeah, that's what it is—then I need to capture the essential music of our time, right? How long *is* our time? A year? A decade? A century? A millennium?

A millennium is too long. A year is too short. Some people live for a hundred years, so I think I'll go with the music of a century. Maybe the top hit songs of each decade from the last hundred years? That ought to capture the flavor of now. If such a thing is possible.

"Kit?" My brother's voice booms up the stairs. "C'mon, let's shoot some hoops."

I look out the window. It's dark, a drizzling January evening where we'd have to play by street-light, and I don't feel like going out there. "Forget it," I yell back.

Mistake. I hear him pounding up the stairs. My door bursts open, and he's got me in a headlock before I'm even out of my chair. "What's that?" he says. "*Forget it*? You're turning me down, bro? Eh? You think?"

Crap. My tattoos. If he starts pounding on my back, I'm toast. "Get off me, jerk!" I twist out of his grasp and glare at him.

He gives me his lopsided grin and holds up his hands, palms out. "Whoa. Sorry. Didn't know I was messing with a tough guy."

"Shut up," I say.

His brows shoot upward. "*Shut up*? You, little brother, are telling me, big brother, to shut up? That's a penalty. Noogie or wedgie?"

"Jeez. Give me a break, Fred. I don't want to shoot hoops, okay?"

"Why not? What else are you doing? And don't give me some bull about homework. More like checking out the action online, maybe?"

"That's only for desperate losers like you."

His grin returns. "Nope. I got a real live one."

"Seriously?"

"Yeah. Her name's Jen and she's in my history class. Smart, beautiful, the perfect woman. For me, the perfect man."

I snort. "As if."

"What, you don't think I'm the perfect man? Okay, so you can't admit it. I understand. That whole jealousy thing, I can handle it. The main thing is, *she* thinks so."

"So is that why you're never around anymore?"

Fred pretends offence. "Kit, you know how much work college is. You think I spend all my time fooling around? *Moi*? No way. The college dude has to study, man." He raises a freedom-fighter fist for emphasis. "Study."

"Yeah, right. Tell me another one."

"Haven't got any more." He flops onto my bed. "So what's new with you?"

I stare at him. "Did Mom put you up to this? You spying for her?"

He frowns. "What are you talking about?"

I turn away. "Nothing."

"No? So who pissed in your cornflakes today?"

"Nobody. Jeez." I shouldn't have said that about spying. He's still looking at me like I've got two heads. Time to change the subject. "Hey, do you remember when we went hiking in Strathcona Park last summer?"

"Yeah. What about it?"

"We're studying mountain climates in geography, and I was thinking, some of those mountains, up past the glacier, they had snow on them in the summer, right?"

"For sure. There was that one, Puzzle Mountain, that still had lots of snow. Some of the other ones did too."

"Does that happen every year? Or does it all melt sometimes?"

Fred shrugs. "I don't know for sure. No, wait. Didn't that park ranger say some of the mountains always have snow year-round?"

"That's what I thought."

"Doesn't it tell you this stuff in your textbook?"

I shake my head. "Nope. We're supposed to do a report on our own mountain-climate experience. Pretty lame, huh?"

Fred yawns. "Beats writing a Shakespearean sonnet."

"Uh. Yeah. Is that what you're doing?"

"Nope. If memory serves, that's what you get to do toward the end of English Twelve." He smirks.

I almost tell him that won't be happening but catch myself in time. Instead I ask, "You don't still have your sonnet lying around by any chance, do you?"

He shakes his head. "Kit, trust me. You wouldn't want to use it. You'd barf. I was heavily under the influence of Xbox at the time and I got an F."

I grin at him. "You wrote a sonnet about Xbox?"

"Don't ask."

Mom's voice rises from the kitchen. "Boys. Dinner. Now."

We take the stairs at double time and skid into the kitchen together. Dad's there, smiling his slow smile, and together we sit down and eat Mom's pasta special with green salad and buttery garlic bread. It's like the clock went back a year; it's that easy and that ordinary. We talk: Dad about the big plumbing contract he's landed, Fred about his car needing new tires, Mom about a case where some guy is suing the parents of a kid who wrote his initials in the guy's new cement walkway.

I don't realize how strange this meal is until it's over. Then Fred heads out, Mom takes off for the gym, Dad settles into his chair in front of the TV and I'm back in my room, facing the computer. For no reason at all, I feel like crying. I don't cry. I just wonder how I went back like that, into my old skin. It's as though I experienced a weird sort of time warp, a strange collision of before and after. Before what? I shake my head, try to get rid of the elusive sense that the world is shifting. I should know what I have to do.

When Ike shows up, he can tell right away that I'm confused, maybe even having second thoughts. "You're not wimping out, are you, Kit? C'mon, man. This is your chance to be somebody. You've got no chance if you don't go through with it."

four

I'm at school, standing at my locker and trying to decide whether I can handle going to my science class, when Ben stops by. He says, "Hey, Kit. How's it going?"

I shrug. "It's going."

"Yeah? Good. So what are you doing tonight?"

"Tonight?"

"Yeah. Friday night, you know? Thought you might like to go with me and the other guys. We're thinking about seeing a movie. Then maybe hang out at Joel's place. Like old times."

I see Ben talking to me. I hear him. But there's this strange barrier between us, like a sheet of ice. Freaky. I look down the hallway, swallow hard and manage to grunt, "Yeah."

Ben says, "Yeah? For sure? That would be great. You want to meet us there, say around seven thirty?"

"Seven thirty."

Ben hesitates. "You okay, Kit?"

I reach into my locker and grab my science text. "Fine. You?" I glance his way and find him frowning.

He says, "I'm good. So, we'll see you tonight, right?"

I nod. He starts walking off, but I catch him looking at me over his shoulder. I half raise my hand, and another kid barreling past knocks into me. It's just enough of a hit to force me to take a step to rebalance, and my locker door connects with my back. My tattoo. The skin feels tight where it's scabbing, and bashing into the door hurts. I can't afford to wreck my tattoo. "Asshole!" I yell.

A teacher appears out of nowhere. "That sort of language is unacceptable. It's Kit Latimer, isn't it?"

I don't look at her. I don't say anything. This is too much.

"Well?" she says.

She's looking for me to say something. What? I know. "Sorry," I mutter.

"Hmph," she snorts. And she leaves.

I leave too. I've got to check on my tattoo. And I have plenty of other stuff to get done. Soon. Real soon.

. . . .

The first thing I do when I get home is take off my shirt and go into the bathroom, twisting myself like a pretzel to see my back in the mirror. It looks wrong, maybe because I'm twisted. The twisting pulls my skin, and the tattooed area feels tight. I grab a hand mirror from one of the bathroom drawers and look again. The letters seem okay, but there's something funny about the lines and dots. I never noticed this when Tony showed me his work in the dingy mirror at his shop. I was distracted because he was telling me to keep it covered with gauze for a day, then put on lotion to heal the scabbing. I should put on some lotion.

But those lines and dots. I look in the mirror again, and now I'm certain Tony did something weird; the tattoos are in a pattern. I didn't ask for a pattern. I don't even think I asked for lines and dots on my back. It must be a code. For what? I don't want to show Ike because he'll tell me I'm an idiot, and I can't show anyone else.

I shift around for a different angle and drop the hand mirror. It shatters into silver shards, scatters all over the tiles. Seven years bad luck, just like that. Hilarious. Is there such a thing as bad luck when you're dead? What could possibly go wrong after that?

Whoa. I know. Wild animals could eat me. A coyote, a wolf, a bear. Or those birds that like shiny stuff—ravens?—they might take my artifacts. Crap. I'll have to hide my body. How do I do that? *Snap!* I know. I'll dig a tunnel into the snow, crawl in and collapse the entrance behind me. Wait till Ike hears about this—he'll be impressed.

The tattoos on my back tingle: they feel like bugs crawling on my skin. Creepy. I've got to put lotion on, lots. That'll help with the scabbing, sure, but it'll smother the lines and dots too. I find some of Mom's lotion and gob it on. The tingling intensifies and starts stinging like crazy, so I pile on more lotion. Man. It takes a while, but finally the sensation subsides.

I head for my computer and pull up the list of artifacts. Here's what I have so far:
- *Blackberry*
- *books—Which ones? Check best-seller list*

- *music of the century—to be loaded into Blackberry*
- *laptop computer with documents saved to hard drive, including my manifesto, Ötzi's story, video of current events and popular games*
- *video of me on Blackberry (Ike's idea)*
- *some sort of food—maybe popular fast food? Hah. Some of that stuff never rots, even when it's not frozen*
- *my sports-card collection (sealed in Baggies), a baseball, a ball cap, Lego*
- *my fossilized seashells that I found in Alberta (so cool to think the ocean was once in Alberta)*
- *one of those portable solar-energy panel devices*
- *myself as artifact: normal clothes that a guy my age wears, including boxers, socks, jeans, T-shirt, hoodie, heavy jacket, gloves, tuque and hiking boots*
- *vodka*

We've already got the vodka—took it from my parents' liquor cupboard. Ike said it wasn't stealing because it was in my house, and what was the difference between that and a peanut-butter sandwich? We argued about that, but in the end, he won. It's hidden in the back of my closet.

I haven't decided on my last two meals. When my corpse is examined, they're going to find out what I ate. When the scientists analyzed Ötzi's intestines, they found out what he ate for his last two meals; one meal was mountain-goat meat and the other some kind of deer meat. Both meals included grain, roots and fruits. The grain might even have been in the form of bread, something the scientists were a bit pumped about since it showed how long people have been making the stuff. They even analyzed his hair to learn what else had been in his diet in the last few months of his life.

A ripple crawls over my skin. They're going to examine my hair and find out what I had for lunch yesterday? Freakin' weird. I wonder if they'll put me into some sort of chemical to preserve me while they do their tests. Maybe formaldehyde, like the cow eyeball we had to dissect in Science 10. The smell of that stuff made me want to puke.

I can't think about that; it's just too bizarre. I look over my artifact list again and decide that had better be it. I'm worried about having enough money to get this stuff, never mind more. I got money from my grandparents for Christmas, and I've got some saved from my job last summer at the golf course, but I might be short. The tattoos and the bus ride to Nanaimo already cost me three hundred bucks.

Another thing that's bugging me—it's only about a half-hour drive from where I live to Strathcona Park, but I can't get a bus to the area I need to go, so I'm going to have to borrow Mom's car. I have my license, but it's like the third degree every time I want to use her car. *Where are you going? Who will be with you? When will you be back?*

I'm not going to get permission to take the car anywhere out of town. No way. But I'm going to have to take it. It's not like I'll damage it. Sooner or later the car will be found in the parking lot up there. Ike says I can't leave a note to tell them where I left it or they'll follow me. I don't know. Mom needs her car to get to work, and she'll be mad at me for screwing up her day, won't she? It would be polite to leave a note.

. . . .

There's quite the scene when Dad comes home and walks into the bathroom. I forgot to clean up the broken mirror, and when he steps on the glass, he starts hollering. He isn't too impressed with the spilled lotion either. Says something about it adding an element of treachery.

"It was an accident," I tell him.

"And you just left it?"

"I forgot about it."

"How can you forget about a thing like that?"

I don't know what to say, and that seems to piss him off even more. He tells me I damn well better get busy and clean it up, pronto. So I start cleaning, but that doesn't stop him from going off some more.

"What's wrong with you, Kit? You've always been a good kid. Kind of a dreamer maybe, but that's another thing. You used to talk about your ideas. How you wanted to get your pilot's license. You were going to build a dune buggy. And a boat. And a house."

He pauses for breath and shakes his head. "You used to build things out of Lego all the time, you and Ben. Haven't seen Ben around for ages. What happened to him?"

I shrug.

"Kit, I dunno what's up with you. You know…all those ideas you had, they were great." He snorts. "But I haven't seen you do a damn thing lately except sit in front of that computer. I've got half a mind to toss the thing out."

"No way!"

"Well, we'll see about that. You just better get with the program—and I'm not talking about the one on the computer."

I swallow the words I want to spew at him, and finally he leaves. I finish cleaning and go straight back to my computer; I need to work on my music list, so I do that for a while. Then I get started on my manifesto.

Manifesto of the Frozen One: Shortly After the Dawn of the Third Millennium AD

To the People of the Future:

My name is Christian Thomas Latimer, but most people call me Kit. I am seventeen years of age and I live in the town of Courtenay on Vancouver Island, in the province of British Columbia. British Columbia is part of the country currently known as Canada, which is on the continent of North America. On planet Earth.

By the time you read this, these places may not exist. I'll bet the names will have changed. Part of me even wonders if the land itself will still be here. Vancouver Island (I'd like to name it Luline after a green-tailed comet) is situated alongside a major fault in the Earth's crust. Some scientists think that if a major earthquake were to occur here, this island would be wiped out.

I've decided to take my chances with that because it seems to me there is no 100% safe place on the planet for a human to preserve his body and his artifacts for five thousand years.

I'm here (wherever HERE is) to create a time capsule for the future. Another man, whose real name we will never know, died on a mountain on the continent of Europe five thousand years ago, and when his mummified corpse was discovered, we learned a lot about life back then. I'm certain it will be just as fascinating for you to know about life in the early part of the third millennium AD, so I have deliberately selected some contemporary artifacts and am willingly laying down my body in a place where I hope it will remain for a long time.

I think you will be pleased to hear from me because maybe it will help you see where you're going when you know where you've been.

That other man on the mountain was nicknamed Ötzi, and in honor of his memory, I've had his name tattooed on my back. It's quite possible that you won't be able to read it (my skin is probably quite withered by now), but if you're wondering about my tattoo, that's what it says. I also have dots and lines tattooed on my back, behind my left knee, and on my right ankle because Ötzi had tattoos in those places. In his case, no one knows why he had them, but there is speculation that it was done to mark his rite of passage into manhood or even as a form of acupuncture (sticking needles in) because X-rays show he may have had arthritis in those joints.

I am hoping that this, my manifesto, will survive so you will know even more about me than we were able to learn about the original Ice Man. I'm also hoping you will find me frozen above a glacier on a mountain that has, for millennia, remained snow-covered, but there's no guarantee. I can only hope.

fiVE

Ike turns up at his usual time, right after dinner, and he's in a weird mood. For the first while, all he says is "Ooga chucka, ooga chucka," over and over again. I crank up the sound on my computer to drown him out, and he finally stops.

"What's the matter, Kit?"

"You're really annoying."

"Oooh. Nasty. Ooga chucka."

"Jeez. Will you stop already? I want you to check out my music list. I've got some jazz from the twenties, some Gershwin and big-band stuff from the thirties, Bing Crosby plus R & B from the forties..."

"They had R & B in the forties?" Ike snorts. "You sure about that?"

"I'm sure. I found a university site that lists this stuff."

"Yeah? So what else have you got?"

"Okay, I've got Elvis Presley tunes plus some Broadway music for the fifties. The sixties had a lot of different styles, so I've included more from that decade. The Beatles, folk stuff, plus some acid rock. And that's as far as I've got."

"That's it?" Ike asks.

"It takes a while, you know. I have to do the research first, then pick the songs, then wait for them to download, then—"

"Okay, okay, I get it. Listen, I've thought of a few more things you should take."

"No, Ike, I don't—"

He cuts me off. "Would you pay attention here for one minute, Kit? Can you do that for me? Thank you. All right, it's like this. You're getting ordinary stuff that's all about an average guy. It's boring. Plus it's discriminatory."

"Discriminatory? What do you mean?"

Ike sighs. "It means you're ignoring the kind of stuff that plenty of guys I know would have with them if they keeled over and croaked. If you weren't such a nerd, you'd know what I mean."

I cross my arms and lean back in my chair. "You're a real jerk, you know that?"

"Yeah? Well maybe I can't help it. Maybe I didn't grow up in a home where Mom cooks dinner every night. Where I get my own computer and people just give me money and I'm so blind to the rest of the world I think my life is normal."

"I don't think I'm normal," I tell him.

"No? Well you are. You're so normal you're scary. You don't think outside the box, man."

"Really? And you do?"

"I don't have a choice. Life hasn't been a cushy ride for me. I've had to learn to think on my feet since day one. And I'm telling you, Kit, you need to consider the less fortunate."

"Okay, so let's say you've got a point. It's true: the stuff I'm planning to bring along is high tech and pricey. I don't even know if I can afford it all. But here's *my* point. What would poor people have that I don't?"

Ike snickers. "Did I say I was talking about poor people? I wasn't. I was talking about people who aren't sucks. Guys who keep a few condoms in their wallets. Not that they'd want to use them if they didn't have to, but they'd have them for show, right?

And they'd have a couple Baggies too. And one of those bags would hold weed and the other would have, oh, let's say E. Or meth."

I can't believe it. "You think I should pack weed and meth? You're crazy. Forget it."

"Fine," he says. "I'll forget it. But you're not going to be a very convincing Ice Man. You're going to betray your times. If you don't have stuff like that, it's like leaving a false trail. Painting a fake picture. 'Cause real people do that stuff. Sex and drugs, man. Sex and drugs."

"Maybe some people. Not me."

"No, not the perfect Kit. Never. I can't believe you're such an idiot. I'm not saying you should *do* the stuff, man. Just have it with you. Let the future know about our social problems. Seems only right. Honest. Not that sex is exactly a social problem. You ever had sex?"

"None of your business."

"So you haven't, eh? Shit. That means you're going to die a virgin."

There's silence as we ponder this. The face of my old girlfriend, Melissa, floats into my mind's eye. Maybe if we'd stayed together...

But then Ike is saying, "Hey, no big. You remember the Ice Man had no penis?"

I come back to the present with a jolt. "God. You're not saying that I..."

"Shit, no. I'm not saying you should whack off your dick." Ike laughs. "That would be crazy. All I'm saying is that maybe Ötzi was a virgin too."

For some reason, this makes me feel better about my virgin status. "Yeah, maybe he was. Or maybe that part just didn't survive five thousand years. But they did say something about how he might have been infertile, didn't they?"

"That's right. And because of that, they thought he could have been some sort of social outcast. Just like you."

I shake my head. "Man, you don't let up, do you?"

"You know what they say. If the shoe fits..." He lets the cliché hang.

I decide to ignore him and turn back to my computer screen. I type in a search for the best-selling books of all time—I don't want the flavor of the week—and am stunned to see what appears as number one.

"Can you believe this? The best-selling book of all time is the Bible."

Ike says, "No way."

"That's what it says on this list. It's sold almost six billion copies."

"Yeah? What does it say for number two?"

"It's *The Little Red Book*, otherwise known as *Quotations from Chairman Mao Tse-tung*. But the note here says that's no surprise since it was compulsory for every Chinese adult to own a copy."

"Oh, right. Chairman Mao was the dude who ran the Cultural Revolution in China, right?"

"How do you know that?" I ask.

Ike snorts. "Why wouldn't I know it? I like documentaries, just like you, remember?"

Right. That's probably the only thing Ike and I have in common. And for sure, he does seem to remember at least as many details as me. Maybe more. He's not all bad.

I go back to the book list. "In the number three slot we have one published in 1783—*The American Spelling Book* by Noah Webster."

"That's gotta be bullshit, man. A spelling book?"

I shrug. "That's what it says."

"Check a different list."

I click back and pick another site. This one shows the same two books in first place, then some other Chinese titles followed by the Koran. "That's strange," I mutter. "How can it be different?"

"Who cares? Just find something that makes sense."

I scan through the titles and find a few I recognize. "Here's *Lord of the Rings*."

"Now you're talking."

"And there's *Harry Potter*. And—"

Ike cuts in. "Is this necessary? I don't care what all the best-selling books are. Just pick the ones you're going to bring."

"That's what I'm trying to do."

"Well you're not going to bring some spelling crap that was published two hundred years ago, are you? That's stupid."

"Okay, okay. You're right. But how am I supposed to decide?"

"Just pick the ones you like. Or the ones from the last hundred years, like the music."

"Yeah, I guess. But I should probably bring the Bible, even though it's—what—two thousand years old, right?"

Ike considers, then says, "Sure. Why not? Makes ·sense, considering how many of our laws and traditions come from there. Plenty of problems too."

"What kind of problems?"

"You know. Religious wars and stuff. Wouldn't it be funny if the dudes in the future got into an argument over it and started fighting?"

"That's retarded. The Bible didn't start any wars. People started them because they came up with different interpretations of what it says."

"There you go. Either way, it's subversive."

"You're nuts."

Ike laughs. "Look who's talking."

I take a deep breath. "This from the guy who just five minutes ago told me I was normal?"

"That's right. I did, didn't I? And you sure managed to change the topic, didn't you? What about the condoms and the weed and the meth, eh?"

Crap. We're back to that. "Even if I wanted to, how am I supposed to get that stuff?"

"What, you don't think there are condoms in the drugstore? And nobody's selling at your school? It's easy-peasy, man."

He's right, of course. Everyone knows who deals at school, and condoms are a no-brainer. "I'm going to have to explain that stuff in my manifesto," I say.

"Sure. Whatever. But you agree it's important to tell the truth about our society, right?"

I sigh. "Wouldn't it be good enough to just write about it?"

"As if," Ike scoffs. "Why write when you can provide the real thing? What if the hard drive on the computer corrodes and your manifesto is gone? Or even if you write out a copy on some sort of freakin' acid-free paper, it could rot away too, whereas the real thing—it's more likely to last."

"Fine. I'll try to get the real thing."

. . . .

I can't sleep. The stuff on my artifact list goes round and round in my head, and I start thinking about how I'm going to get all of it. I know I don't have enough money. And then I think about Melissa. I still see her at school sometimes. She smiles, but then her eyes slide away and she goes by. It's over three months since we were together, and every time I see her I still get this ache, deep in my gut. I loved her then. I still do. I can still feel the texture of her kitten-soft hair, the smooth lines of her cheeks, the round curve of her hips. I can still smell her, that lemony rose scent she wore. I can taste the strawberry lip gloss and the cinnamon gum she liked to chew.

When she dumped me, she said, "You're the sweetest guy ever, Kit. But it's just, well, we have nothing in common, you know?"

She was wrong. We had sweetness in common. Unless she was lying. And then that would mean I'm not sweet and neither is she for lying, and then we'd have that in common—being un-sweet. Either way, there was something between us. I know there was.

Maybe I should have asked Fred for advice. He always seems to have a girlfriend, so he must know something. I remember this one time, last summer, when we were shooting some hoops. We were just fooling around, not really keeping score or anything, which wasn't like him. He usually played to win, forced me to play up to his level. He's two years older than me and he's always been ahead, always better at most everything.

Still, he hasn't been a bad brother. If it wasn't for him pushing me so hard, maybe I wouldn't have been good enough to make the basketball team. For sure not good enough to be one of the best players. And I have to say, Fred has never let me down. If he said he was going to do something with me, he did it. Like on that day I'm thinking about, I heard him talking to one of his buddies on the phone. Fred said, "The beach? What time?"

Then I heard him say, "No can do. I told Kit I'd shoot some hoops with him."

There was a pause, and he said, "No man, I'm not going to blow him off. Later, okay?"

But when we started playing, it seemed like he wasn't into it, seemed more like he wanted to talk. He asked me how it was going.

I said, "It's going."

"Yeah? Is your team going to make the finals next season?"

"Are you kidding?" I asked.

"So that's a yes. Good stuff. And how's Melissa?"

Man, all I had to do was hear her name and I couldn't stop a smile from landing on my face. I think Fred knew it too, and he'd ask about her just to see me go goofy.

"She's great."

"Great?"

"Yeah. I mean, she's a great person, you know?"

"Cool. Not too hard on the eyes either, eh?"

I gave Fred a look. "That's not why...I mean, she is, but that's not what's important. It's more, uh... It's like she's so..."

I tried to tell him how it wasn't her looks that were so special, but I couldn't get the words out.

My brain just sort of jammed up on me. It used to really bug Melissa when that happened.

Fred laughed and said, "I know, I know. You love her for her mind, right?"

"Yeah," I told him. "And her...her..." I blanked again.

Fred looked at me funny, like he was trying to figure something out. "You okay, Kit?"

"I'm fine."

"Yeah? So what's with the stutter thing?"

"It's not a stutter!"

"No? Maybe not. But something's different. You and your buds smoking weed?"

I shrugged. "We tried it. Who hasn't? But we're not getting to the finals by smoking up, are we? Besides..."

"Besides what?"

"Nothing."

Fred shook his head. "There you go again. Gapping out."

"I wasn't gapping out. I was just going to say I don't like weed anyway. Makes me feel strange."

Fred laughed then. "Stranger than usual you mean?"

I punched Fred's shoulder and said, "Game on." I took a shot, waited for the ball's slide through the hoop and was ready to grab it on the rebound when Fred's long arm swiped in and snatched it away.

"You," Fred said, "are going to pay for that cheap shot. Think you can catch me off guard, huh?"

We played hard for a while then, and it seemed all normal, all good. But if I'd been smart, when he asked about Melissa I'd have told him things weren't perfect with her. I should have asked him what I was doing wrong, and maybe he could have told me. And maybe I'd still be with Melissa.

Six

I see Ben at school on Monday and it's only then that I remember about the movie on Friday night. He strides right past me in the hall, shaking his head like he just saw something disgusting.

I call after him. "Ben?"

He doesn't stop.

Jeez, how did I forget about the movie? Right. I hung out with Ike and got so busy with the research and planning…I feel like a jerk. But then, maybe it's better this way. It's not like I can tell Ben what I'm doing; if we hung out together, I could slip up. And he's not going to miss a loser who never keeps his word either, right?

It's definitely better this way.

I drift through my English class, then go to art. Instead of letting us draw, the teacher, Ms. Thorpe, gives us a slide show of famous works of art. This is good because I can just prop my chin in my hands and keep my face there and that's it. There was a time when I might have been pissed off about not being able to work on one of my boat drawings, but I haven't started anything new lately, and Ms. Thorpe's been on my case about that.

I'm watching the slides flash by, just starting to think I should include some pictures of modern art to show to the future, when along comes this slide of a naked dude sculpted in white marble. A couple of idiots start sniggering about his dick, and suddenly I'm hearing what the teacher is saying.

"This is Michelangelo's *David*. It's considered by many to epitomize perfect male beauty. Stunning, isn't it?" She pauses to give us time to study the sculpture, and then she says, "A few years ago I read about a disorder dubbed the 'David Syndrome.' It seems that when some especially sensitive people view this piece, or other extraordinarily beautiful works of art, they're overcome with emotion."

"What happens to them?" a girl asks.

"I don't recall all the specifics, but I believe the viewer initially experiences deep wonder. Do any of you feel that way?"

I stare at the statue and get nothing. It's just an image on a projection screen.

"Anybody?" Ms. Thorpe asks.

The same girl giggles and says, "Well, he is pretty hot."

More sniggers erupt but Ms. Thorpe cuts in. "I'd be surprised if you did. It only happens with the original artwork. The peculiar thing is that after the viewer feels wonder, they often get panicky and then disoriented and aggressive. At that point, they may attempt to attack the work of art. In fact, a number of years ago, one man actually succeeded in doing considerable damage to one of David's feet with a hammer."

"Weird," someone says. "Why?"

"It's difficult to say. Something in the extreme beauty disorients them. Some experience hallucinations. Quite a few people have even been temporarily hospitalized until their emotions are under control."

"I don't get it," the girl says. "If you think something is beautiful, why would you want to wreck it? Doesn't make sense."

"No," Ms. Thorpe says, "it doesn't. But I wanted to mention it because I think it illustrates how powerful art can be."

I don't hear the rest of the exchange. I just keep staring at David until she flips to the next slide, and I'm still stuck back there, thinking about how crazy people can be. I glance around the art room and realize that any one of these people could be insane. How can I tell which one? I can't. On the surface, they just look like a bunch of kids.

Suddenly it's lunchtime, and I figure I should go check out the bush area behind the parking lot, where the dealers hang out. I'm not ready to buy yet, but the last I heard, that was the place to score. I saunter down there, lean on a tree and wait. My back tattoo starts to itch, and then I get this really weird sensation. It's as if the tattoo is coming to life.

I know it's stupid. A tattoo can't come to life. It's nothing but ink. Unless the ink has something in it. What if Tony mixes nano-size transmitters in his ink? Or nano-robots? How would anyone know? The robots could start crawling around, enter the bloodstream, go into the brain and then...Then Tony could take control of my brain.

I bang my head against the tree trunk, and then I look at the trunk and wonder if maybe it's an oak tree, like those sacred oaks the Druids had. Did they plant them or just find them in the forest? Who planted this tree? I'm studying the tree, trying to figure it out, when a group of stoners slouches by. One of them snickers; he sounds almost exactly like Ike. I whip my head around and look at them, and someone says, "Talk about your freak shows. You trippin' or what?"

I stare at him and say nothing.

Another guy says, "Him? No way. Isn't he one of the jocks from the basketball team?"

"Whatever, man. Who knows? Who cares?"

And they're gone. And the strange sensation is still there. It's like a buzz, a drone, and with absolute clarity I realize it's exactly the same sound made by Tony's tattoo machine.

I start running. I don't stop until I'm home. The first thing I do is strip off my shirt and check my back. The tattoo is coated with a thin layer of scabbing. Maybe the nanos are in the scabs? And maybe the buzz is them warming up before they're released into my bloodstream. If I'm lucky, that could be it. I scratch at the scabs and little chunks break off. I scratch harder, and then there's blood. That's good, because the nanos will be flushed out with the blood. I strip off the rest of my clothes and get into the shower, letting the hot water pound on my back while I scrub at it with one of Mom's loofahs.

After a while, the loofah is covered in black scabs and blood, and my back feels like it's on fire. I don't care. The buzz has stopped; I've beaten Tony. No way for him to take control of my brain now. I get out of the shower, towel off and rub lotion into my raw back, lots of lotion. I'm careful to make sure there isn't any lotion left on the floor, and I take every-thing—the bloody towel, my clothes, the loofah—and toss it into the washing machine.

I'm really tired. Almost no sleep for the past few nights and then this…I crawl into bed, and the next thing I know, Mom is leaning over me.

"Kit? Kit? Are you sick? The school called to say that you missed some classes today."

Her presence startles me. I bolt upright and ask, "What the hell are you doing here?"

She takes a step back. "Excuse me? Do you think you might want to rephrase that question?"

I stare at her. "What?"

She sighs, reaches out and places the back of her hand on my forehead. "You do feel a bit warm."

I'm suddenly aware of my tattoo; it's hot and sticky. I lie back and say, "Yeah?"

"Is your stomach bothering you? Have you been throwing up? I noticed you put your clothes in the wash."

"Yeah. I, uh, puked and thought I better clean up."

"Well, that was considerate. I'll give the school a call tomorrow and let them know you were ill. Aren't you supposed to sign out at the office or something, so they know?"

I nod. "Sorry. I felt lousy and just left."

"I see." Her brow furrows. "Well, how are you feeling now? Do you want me to bring you a glass of water or some soup?"

"Soup would be good."

"You think it'll stay down?"

"I think so."

Her brow smoothes and she smiles, her lips curving up only at the edges. I love that smile. It's the one that always seems like it was made just for me. "All right. I'll go make the soup. Chicken noodle okay?"

"For sure. Thanks, Mom."

I get the smile again, and then she's gone.

I reach around and feel my back. Damn. It must have kept oozing. I'm going to have to wash my sheets now too, but I can't do that while Mom's in the house. Seems like she notices every little thing. Guess I'll have to act sick enough to stay home from school again tomorrow just so I can wash the sheets.

Dad brings me the soup. "Hey, guy, not feeling so good?"

I nod.

"That's too bad. Maybe a stomach bug or something got you, eh?"

A stomach bug? A bug in my stomach? Oh. He means *that* sort of bug. I'm not really sick, not at all. It's just the tattoo. I shrug and say, "I guess."

I wait for him to leave, but he doesn't. Instead he sits down on my desk chair and stretches out his legs. "Seems like we haven't talked much lately, Kit. How's everything going?"

"Good." I take a mouthful of soup. I hope he gets his little visit over with fast.

"Glad to hear it. School going all right?"

"Fine."

"Good, good. So, what about basketball? When's your next game?"

Basketball. What's with everyone bringing up basketball? I haven't thought about it for a while. Things went wonky with it this year. When the season started in October, I went out for the team as usual, and for the first while everything was okay. But by December, I sucked. It was horrible. I'd go to do a layup and trip over my own feet. I'd drop the ball, miss catching it, was lucky to get a shot off, never mind score. The coach was freaking, trying to talk to me, telling me to get my head in the game, giving me extra drills...nothing helped.

The other guys were okay with it at first, slapped my back, said stuff like "too bad" or "that was bum luck" or "c'mon, Kit, you just gotta focus, man." But after I let them down a few more times, they weren't so supportive. I started getting dirty looks and they stopped talking to me and I...Well, I stopped caring about it. When school started up after the winter break, I didn't go back to basketball.

Dad says, "Kit? When's the game? If it's an evening one, I'd like to come and watch."

Shit. I try stalling. "I don't know. I think it's next week."

He frowns. "Not until then? That's funny. The finals are coming up in March." His frown deepens. "Come to think of it, you haven't mentioned the team lately. How are you doing in the standings?"

I give him a look. "I quit."

His mouth gapes and he shakes his head. "You *quit*? When?"

I shrug. "A week or so ago."

"What the hell! Why?"

"I sucked."

Dad leans forward and squints at me. Finally, he says, "Kit, I've watched those boys play for years, and I know darn well you're one of the best."

"Not anymore."

"Is there something you're not telling me?"

"What do you mean?"

"I mean maybe they've got some rules about academic standing? Your grades were sliding on your last report card. If they aren't acceptable, you can't play?"

"My grades are fine." That's probably a lie, but by the time the next report card comes out, I won't be around to worry about it.

And then his face goes white. He stares at me, all weird, and says, "You're doing drugs, aren't you?"

"*What?*"

"That would account for everything. Sweet Jesus, Kit. How could you? You know better."

"Yeah. I *do* know better. I'm *not* doing drugs, Dad. You think I'm stupid? Jeez, maybe I *should* do them if that's what you think."

He keeps his eyes glued to mine, and then slowly, gradually, he eases back. He passes a hand over his face, and when it's gone, he looks older, tired. "I don't know," he mutters. "Doesn't seem like you're lying, but none of this makes sense to me, Kit."

I look away from him.

"Come on, Kit. Talk to me. What's going on?"

I can't look at him. I spoon a mouthful of soup into my mouth and it tastes terrible, like it was made with sweaty socks. "This is gross." I lean back on my pillows and close my eyes.

He's quiet for a few minutes. Then he sighs and says, "Sorry. Guess I shouldn't come down on you when you're under the weather. But I think I'll have a talk with your coach."

I keep my eyes shut and mutter, "Whatever." The coach probably had the same idea, but I deleted the messages he left on the phone.

"Damn it, Kit. I'm worried about you."

"Don't be."

"Can't help it. You'll understand when you're a father someday."

I open my eyes and say, "I won't be..." I stop.

Dad smiles. "No, not for a long while, you won't. At least, I hope not." He gets quiet again, then says,

69

"Hey, you know what? There's a documentary on TV tonight about a tomb they just discovered in Egypt, in the Valley of the Kings. Sounds like a good one, eh? We should watch it."

Dad and his documentaries. They're his favorite thing on TV. He got me hooked on them years ago, and we used to watch a few every week. History, science, nature, we watched them all. Seems like we haven't done that lately. "Sure," I say. "I mean, if I'm feeling all right by then, I'll come down."

"Good stuff."

After he leaves, I finish most of the soup, then nod off into a half sleep. Later, I hear Dad come in again, telling me it's time for the show. I keep my eyes closed, my breathing even. He steps into my room, moves to my desk, and I hear the shuffle of papers. What is he doing? He's snooping around like a sneak thief. How dare he go nosing through my things! My muscles clench, and I'm about to launch from the bed, confront him, tell him to get the hell out, when he sighs and steps toward my bed. He pauses, and I swear I can feel his eyes gazing down at me. I'm going to explode any second now—*boom, splat*— but somehow I remain still.

"Kit?" he murmurs.

I don't react. He sighs again, picks up the soup bowl and moves to the door. He switches off the light, and a moment later the door closes softly behind him. I heave my own sigh, and my tight muscles go limp. I feel weak. Maybe I really am sick. Funny how pretending something can make it feel real.

Or maybe I'm just in really bad shape. Playing basketball used to keep me fit. It was there, on the court last year, that I first saw Melissa. She was new in town, and she'd joined the cheerleading squad. It was the craziest thing, because she zeroed in on me, out of all the guys on the team. I could feel her gaze following me, and every time I glanced in her direction, our eyes met.

I'd look away fast, stay cool, keep my head in the game. At least, that's what I told myself. I told myself I was imagining it; she wasn't after me, she couldn't be, not *this* girl. She seemed so different from the others. It didn't feel like she was just trying to get me to notice her because I was a basketball star, a status symbol. That's how it was for some of the guys and their girlfriends; they went around posing, showing off to everyone what perfect couples they made.

But with Melissa, when our eyes met, it felt like she saw the real me, saw right inside me and liked what she found, wanted to know more. I couldn't stop looking for her, and sure enough, those dark eyes would be waiting, and her smile made me want to see inside her too.

This went on for a while, and then some of the other guys started to notice it too. "Whoo, Kit, that new girl is hot for you." Or "Hey, check it out. Kit has a groupie." And "So, what are you going to do, Kit? Come on, she's yours for the asking. Easy. What're you waiting for? She's got a nice set of…"

"Shut up, will you?" I hated them talking about her like that. She seemed so authentic, not someone the guys should be allowed to trash-talk in the locker room. Some of them did that plenty and I never liked it, but when they started on her, I wanted to stuff the basketball down their throats.

I went out of the locker room that day, still feeling the heat of the game in my muscles and the heat of anger toward those guys, and there she was, hanging out with a couple of other girls. I started walking past, and she said, "Hey. You're Kit, aren't you?"

I stood there and she said some other things, but I have no idea what because I just drank her in, and pretty soon we were walking along, just the two of us.

It was getting dark, and we looked up and saw the moon rising, a crescent moon, and I said, "Do you ever look at it and think about how astronauts went up there and planted flags?"

She laughed and shook her head, and I felt like an idiot, but then she took hold of my hand, and hers felt so small and warm. That was it. I was hers.

SEVEN

They are the size of bacteria, invisible to the naked eye. They number in the thousands: tiny, perfectly engineered, mindless. When released in the bloodstream, the nano-bots circulate freely, each propelled like a jet by capacitors generating magnetic fields that pull conductive fluids through one end of an electromagnetic pump and shoot it out the other end. They carry weapons, not of mass destruction, but of minute destruction.

Some have probes. Others are armed with minuscule knives and chisels capable of hacking away at bits of matter the size of nanometers. One nanometer is equal to one billionth of a meter, almost nothing. But just as the sea can grind rock to dust, one particle at a time, the power of the nano-bots is not in their numbers but in their persistence.

There are other weapons. Electrodes, in pairs, can generate a current. Tiny lasers can burn away material. Cavities within the robots can carry chemicals. How much? Almost nothing.

"Almost" is of the utmost importance. Much like the difference between dead and almost dead.

The nano army is awash in black ink. The ink is composed of magnetite crystals, powdered jet, wustite, bone black, and amorphous carbon from combustion (soot). Now the army is immersed in a chemical mixture of water, amino acids, proteins, carbohydrates, lipids, hormones, vitamins, electrolytes, dissolved gases (oxygen, carbon dioxide and nitrogen) and cellular wastes. In other words, blood.

The army is entirely aimless. It must await the direction of a powerful magnet, one that, when wielded, will attract the unquestioning to follow. The army is not really invisible; if one were to examine the country it has invaded with an MRI machine, its presence could be detected. If one wished to withdraw the troops, they could be retrieved via a magnetic homing device, positioned at one of several portals: the throat, for example.

I rise out of sleep in spastic leaps. My mind grasps at the shards of the craziest, scariest, most amazing dream of my life. Such incredible detail! At the same time, my mind wants out of there, to be free of the nightmare, to waken and shed the clinging bits swimming with me into consciousness.

My eyes snap open and roam the familiar comfort of my bedroom, and I groan with relief. But I need to remember. It was important, I know; almost as if my dreaming mind was superintelligent and playing a special documentary, just for me. I sit up and every movement of my body, every ordinary object my brain registers, is a step away from remembering.

Then Mom comes in. "How are you today, Kit? Feeling better?"

I gaze at her, struggling to understand why she's asking this question. Does she know about my dream?

"Kit? Are you still sick?" She strides toward me, and there's that hand on the brow again. "Hmmm. You feel a touch warm, but I wouldn't say you have a fever."

Right. I'm sick. I was throwing up yesterday, wasn't I? And there's something else, something to do with blood.

"Maybe I should get the thermometer and we'll take your temperature."

I shake my head. "No." She is not sticking anything down my throat. No way.

Mom raises her eyebrows. "So you're better? You're going to school?"

"No."

"Kit…" She frowns. "Why are you looking at me like that?"

"Like what?"

"I don't know. Like you…hate me."

I stare at her.

She takes a deep breath. "Sorry. I didn't mean that. Hate is a terrible word. It's just that you look so angry. All I suggested was taking your temperature. That's not a crime, is it?"

"Mom. Forget it. You're making a big deal out of nothing."

"Am I? I wonder if I should make an appointment for you with the doctor. You just don't seem like yourself these days, Kit."

"I'm *fine*, okay? Jeez. It's just a freakin' stomach bug." A stomach bug. A fragment of my dream surfaces, and I concentrate, trying to catch it.

"Just the same, it wouldn't hurt to see the doctor."

The fragment shatters beyond recognition. "I'm *not* going to the doctor."

She folds her arms across her chest. "So you're going to school?"

"Mom. I'm not feeling good, okay? Not good enough to go to school. But that doesn't mean I'm sick enough to go to the doctor. Since when should people go to the doctor for every little thing? Isn't that what you always say?"

She opens her mouth like she's going to say something but snaps it shut again. She glances at her watch and then back at me. "Fine. If I don't get moving now I'm going to be late, but this discussion isn't over. We'll talk more later."

I shrug. "Whatever."

"Kit!" Her voice has that warning note, the one she always uses when she's close to launching into a marathon tirade.

"Okay, okay. Later."

By the time she's gone and the house is quiet, I've completely lost my dream. I throw my sheets in the wash, eat toast with peanut butter and jam, and finally remember what started all this. My tattoo.

I check it in the mirror and it's a mess of ink and raw, oozing scabs. I really screwed up the word *Ötzi*. It looks more like *Clzi* now. Crap. I wonder how much it'll cost to get it fixed, but there's no way I'm going back to any tattoo parlor. No damn way. I should never have gone there in the first place, and going again would be sheer suicide.

Suicide. What a joke. Isn't that what I'm doing? Or is it? Why do people kill themselves anyway? I guess they can't stand living anymore, but that's not what it's about for me. I'm doing it for posterity. More like a martyr. A hero even.

I won't tell Ike that I think this whole deal is heroic because I know he'll laugh, but it makes me feel good to see it in this light. Doesn't this mission require courage? Isn't it about self-sacrifice for the greater good of humanity?

It's time I got back to work on my manifesto, but I'm stumped. How do I explain life as I know it? When the manifesto was just in my head it seemed so clear, but now it seems vast and chaotic. Maybe I need categories. But what categories? School is broken down into separate subjects. Should I use those? English, math, science, geography, history... that seems so lame.

Wait a minute. It's obvious. Education is a category. What else? Work. And the basic stuff it takes to live, like food and shelter. Those are categories too. I pull up the document on my computer and start writing.

Category One: Language

I am worried that you won't be able to read this. Even though plenty of people speak English today, it's a language that keeps changing. Also, it's the language that started out in England and was originally spoken by mostly Caucasian (white) people, but maybe there won't be any more Caucasians left in another thousand years or so. We're not breeding as much as other races, and there are lots of inter-racial marriages, fine by me, maybe there won't be any separate races at all. This is a good thing because it will likely stop people from having stupid problems about something as superficial as skin color.

Human sexuality seems foggy now, with gay and bi people it's like the edges are blurred. Plus there are advances in science with stuff like cloning and test tube babies etc., so maybe there won't be such a thing as male and female anymore since who will need that for reproduction? This is relevant to language because............in English, people are divided into male and female by the language. We don't have a word for someone in between him or her. It's one or the other. Turkish and Tagalog don't have this problem. I'll bet English will get that way too.

Maybe it's not going to be a problem for you after all because I'm not going to talk about that anyway. For the record, I know a little French because we have to take that in school, but I don't know enough of any other language besides English. I could make up a language like J.R.R. Tolkien did (his books were mega-best-sellers). He made up Elvish. Elves are a different race, sort of like humans with pointy ears (like Mr. Spock), but they've all gone to the far green country. I don't know where that is. It could be Ireland? Or the planet Vulcan. They went by beautiful boats, and I did think of making one like that.

Category Two: Education

I have been partially educated by our public school system. I've learned about reading, writing, Math, science, computers, history, and geography. A lot of this is useful, and there are plenty of places where kids don't get a proper education. In some places, little kids have to work or even join armies, and some girls don't go to school. Just because they're girls. Very weird.

I guess education is okay, but there are many things they don't teach us. We don't learn how to grow food in case the whole system collapses due to conspiracies (there are many conspiracies) or anything about what's really going on in the world. I think they try to distract us by forcing us to memorize useless facts and maps. Regarding Maps, there is one called the Piri Reis map which was made in Constantinople in AD 1513. It shows the coast line of Antarctica very accurately—without ice. Everyone knows ice has covered that coast for thousands of years, so how did that cartographer know what the coast line looked like? It was only in 1949 that a seismic survey could see through the ICE and figure out where the land hidden underneath lies. Piri Reis says he used older maps to make his, but then, who made the older maps? Someone from maybe 6,000 years before, when the ice wasn't there, right? And who was that?

It was the civilization from long ago and they just ignore it in school because for some reason they don't want us to know that an advanced civilization was here before and it mostly got wiped out. How? Who knows some people think it was a massive flood, like the one in the bible. In some ways I'm sorry that I won't be getting further education there are a lot of things I'd like to learn more about. However, knowledge is irrelevant when you're dead.

Yeah. A lot of things are irrelevant when you're dead, but I'm not dead yet and I'm hungry. I head down to the kitchen and start poking around in the cupboards. There's some funny stuff. A can of corn that says *Fresh from the Fields*. Gimme a break. There's a jar of dill pickles too, cucumbers preserved in salt water and vinegar. I look at them for a while. They still sort of look like cucumbers. Only now they're pickles. I don't want to eat them. Maybe a sandwich? I'm trying to decide if I want a grilled-cheese sandwich or KD when Ike shows up.

"How did you know I was here?" I ask.

"I checked at your school and since you weren't there, it wasn't too hard to figure out the alternative. What are you doing?"

"Having lunch. Want some?"

"Sure. What are you making?"

"Grilled cheese."

"Sounds good. Then we should get going."

I look up from the bread I'm buttering. "Get going?"

Ike says, "Yup. We're running out of time."

Eight

"How can we be running out of time?" I ask Ike.

He says, "Time is speeding up. You're dragging your sorry ass, and we've got to pick up the pace. Have you got the artifacts?"

I shake my head. "No, man. I've hardly got any. And I'm not done with the music collection or my manifesto..."

"Excuses. I should have known. You're not going through with it, are you? Man, you make me sick."

I feel like crying. I can't cry in front of Ike, no way. But it's too much. All I've been doing is trying to get ready, and now this? I don't answer him. I get the cheese and keep making the sandwiches.

"So you *are* giving up, aren't you?" he asks.

"Go to hell."

"Yeah," he laughs, "I just might. More interesting than hanging around here with a guy who breaks his word. Hey, since you're a liar, I'll probably meet you there, huh?"

"I didn't say I was giving up. I just said I'm not ready."

He sighs heavily. "Okay. So what do you still need? You've got the vodka, the clothes, the computer, the tattoo. It won't take more than a couple hours to do your stupid manifesto, will it? And then finish getting the music and *voilà*. Done."

"Um, Ike. Remember we said we need that Blackberry? Plus, in case you hadn't noticed, my computer isn't a laptop. I have to buy that stuff, plus the solar panel and some books...I was thinking about an atlas too, so they could see what the map of the world looks like now. And then there's the drugs and the condoms. Man, I don't think I have enough money for everything."

"What? Now you're telling me you don't have the money? That's bullshit."

"So I don't, what can I say?"

"You think your parents or Fred would lend you some cash?"

"No. They know I've got money, and if I ask for more, they're going to ask me what it's for." I laugh. "You think I can tell them?"

"Okay. Here's what we're going to do. We're just going to get the stuff."

"How?"

"Take it. What else?"

I feel sick. I know what he's saying. "You think I'm going to steal it? No way."

"Way!" he roars. "Get your head on straight, will you? We need this stuff for science, man. For the future. It's not for us, it's for them. You're going to get it."

"No," I say. My voice comes out shaky and whiny. "No."

"How much money have you got?" he asks.

I ponder. "I think around four hundred bucks."

Ike snorts. "Really? A lousy four hundred? Well, well, you sure sucked me in, didn't you?"

"What do you mean?"

"I mean all this big talk, like you could actually go through with it, when you knew all along you couldn't. You were just playing me, weren't you, Kit?"

"No. I fully intend to do it. I just didn't realize... I mean, maybe we'll have to cut back. Just take a cheap cell phone and a digital camera. Forget the

GPS and the video and the music. Or I could even leave all the music on my computer, and I'll take that instead of a laptop."

"You're going to haul your friggin' computer up a mountain? You'll be lucky if you make it out of the parking lot."

My mind works furiously. There must be a way. And then I've got it. "I'll take a sled. We have a sled in the garage, and all the stuff will fit on that. I can pull a sled up the mountain, no problem."

Ike whistles. "Wow. You're serious, aren't you? Maybe the sled will work. And maybe you can take your big-ass computer instead of a laptop. So it's going to look like you did this on the cheap, like you didn't really care about preserving state-of-the-art technology..."

"I care about it! I just can't do it, that's all. I'll explain in my manifesto." I hope those guys in the future can read English. I've got a lot of explaining to do about my second-rate stuff.

It's as if Ike reads my thoughts because he says, "So you're really okay with them getting the second-class artifacts? Figures. Goes along with the second-class guy they're getting too." I can't argue with that.

Instead I flip the sandwiches and stare at them in the frying pan, watching the cheese melt and ooze, wondering if any of this will show up in my frozen intestines. Maybe Ike is right, time is speeding up. Everything is happening too fast, and I need to slow it down. I reach out and turn the heat on the stove as low as it will go.

"Tell you what," Ike says. "Let's go to the mall and check out the prices on a few things. We'll figure out how much you can get and then go from there."

So we go to the mall. The first thing Ike wants me to do is withdraw all my money from my account so we know how much cash we've got. I was almost right; I've got $393.

From there, we go to the bookstore and get a Bible for twenty bucks. We look at cell phones and digital cameras and figure out even the craptastic ones would add up to a couple of hundred dollars. We check out laptops; the low-end models are over six hundred.

When we move on to the Blackberries, the guy behind the counter lets me examine one. He shows me all the features, and it's amazing. He says, "Of course, as with all digital recording, some sound quality is lost. But this sacrifice means you can take it with you."

Take it with you? As in those jokes about rich guys who want their money buried with them in their coffins?

No. He just means you can take along the music.

And it's got nothing to do with artifacts.

It's quiet in the store as the guy demonstrates how to use the video, camera and GPS. Then the store phone rings, and he goes to answer it.

"It's perfect," Ike hisses.

"I know," I mutter. "But look at the price tag. Can't afford it."

"So take it."

"What?"

"Right now! He said you can take it with you. He's not even looking at us. He's got his head stuck in a cupboard over there. C'mon, Kit. The future needs it. Let's go!"

I grab it. I don't know how, exactly, but I slide the Blackberry up my sleeve and walk away. Within seconds, we're out of the store. Nothing happens. Within a minute, we're at the mall exit doors. We walk through, slow and cool as anything, then once we're outside we speed up, make for the corner of the building, deke around it, and then we're running. We run across the parking lot, and I think I hear shouts coming from behind us, but we keep going. Pretty soon we're in the park across the street, dodging between the trees, and Ike is laughing like a maniac.

It's only when we're several blocks away that we stop, panting, in front of the bus stop.

"See?" Ike crows. "It was easy. We did it."

I have the urge to throw up. Maybe I do have a stomach bug. I shouldn't be out running around. I let the Blackberry slip from my sleeve into my palm. I stare at it.

"Not here!" Ike says. "Keep it hidden. No one can see this, Kit, you understand? No one!"

I gulp and slide it back up my sleeve. I clench my fingers tight on the fabric, pinching it shut so the Blackberry can't escape.

"I'm going to take off now," Ike says. "Better if we don't stick together. See you later, dude."

And he's gone. I wait at the bus stop, breathing in and out; pretty soon the bus comes along. I get on and have trouble getting my hand into my pants pocket to get my change. I can't let go of my sleeve, can I?

I press my arm close to my body to pin the Blackberry in place and start working my hand down.

The bus driver says, "Got a problem with your arm, kid?"

Does he know? Can he see the bulge in my sleeve? My fingers close around some coins and I withdraw my hand, turn it palm up, but keep my arm clamped to my side.

The driver sighs, reaches into my palm, plucks out the coins he requires and waves me to the back. I go.

I get home and into my room before I bring out the Blackberry, and, man, I hate it. Hate is a strong word, but it's the right word. I really hate it.

I turn it on and it starts beeping. Shit! It's transmitting my location. The GPS...I fumble to find the button to switch it off, and each beep feels like a spike in my brain. When at last it falls silent I drop it on my desk and watch it. Does it need to be turned on to work or does it continue signaling when it's shut off? Was that enough time for them to pinpoint my location?

And then it dawns on me. That was a low-battery warning beep. I heave out a gush of breath I didn't know I was holding and realize I have a problem. I'm going to need a battery charger. Maybe someone's cell-phone charger will work, but I doubt it. And there is no way I'm going back into that store again for as long as I live—which won't be long—but who else sells chargers for these things? Someone must.

Okay, I'm thinking more clearly now. I'll buy a charger—no more stealing no matter what Ike says. I'm just not cut out for that. I can't believe I freaked myself out about the GPS. The guy in the store explained that the Blackberry's satellite receiver only works once you sign up for service and activate the unit. Obviously I won't be doing that.

There's a terrible smell in the house. I noticed it when I ran in, but now it's making me feel nauseous. I start checking around and find the grilled-cheese sandwiches smoking in the frying pan. They look like lumps of charcoal, and the frying pan is warped and totally black. Mom's going to kill me. I look at the clock; it's only 2:00 PM. So much has happened since we forgot to eat the sandwiches that I wonder for a moment if it's 2:00 AM. But no, everyone would have come home and we'd have had dinner...Ike is dead wrong about time speeding up.

I put the frying pan in the sink and run some water over it. Then I put it in a bag and take it outside to the garbage can. I open all the doors and windows, turn on the ceiling fans, spray air freshener everywhere. The house still stinks. I'm lucky it didn't catch on fire.

Fire. Is that the opposite of ice? I haven't thought about fire for a long time. I find one of Mom's scented candles and light it, watch the flame for a while. The scent is nice so I light a few more and figure for sure this will get rid of the stench. One of the candles smells like roses, and in an instant I'm back in time, back with Melissa.

We went to a beach party last fall with some of the other kids from school. We'd been together for around six months, and parties weren't my favorite scene anymore. I wanted to stay home with her, maybe just rent a movie. But she wanted to go, said she'd go without me, so I went.

At first it was all right. People were just sort of milling around in the dark, gathering drift-wood, talking, laughing. Quite a few people had coolers and beer, and those started going around, then a boom box appeared and we had music. The bonfire we got going was huge, and I was content to sit there with my arm around Melissa and watch the flames. I didn't really notice when a few people started dancing, but Melissa tried hauling me to my feet to join in, and I told her to forget it. I didn't want to dance. She got sulky, but I didn't care. I figured it was no big deal, she'd get over it.

Then this guy I didn't know showed up. He hung out for a bit, and the next thing I knew he was doing this amazing stunt, swinging balls of fire around on string.

"Wow," Melissa breathed. "Fire poi. So cool." I looked at her but she wasn't looking back. She was entranced by those spinning balls of fire, mesmerized by their whirling, arcing flight, and maybe by the guy who wielded them too. He had his shirt off and his skin was golden in the firelight. He looked like someone from another place and time, maybe even another species. Someone cranked the music louder and this guy went with it, moving in rhythm with the sound and making the flaming poi, bright against the black night, dance too.

Melissa jumped to her feet, and her body started swaying. I sensed rather than saw that nearly all the kids were dancing now, synchronized with the fire poi, but it was her I watched. And saw. Saw someone there I hadn't seen before, a stranger whose body moved in perfect harmony with the poi dancer's rhythm. I was stunned, disoriented. I tried to get a fix on those dervishes of fire, but I couldn't. No fix at all. They had become an indecipherable blur, a spinning vortex. I got up and took off, running.

I had to get away, far enough away to see only clean, simple black.

I guess I was gone for a while. Melissa never came after me. When I got back, the fire poi show was over, and the kids were a moving mass on the sand, dancing in clumps and pairs. Those in pairs were grinding against each other, and Melissa was part of a pair. With him. The stranger. I stood way back from the light, stood as one with the dark. It was cold in the dark. Very cold.

Cold.

I come back to the present with a jolt and notice it's friggin' freezing in the house. I turn up the furnace and go outside so I can check the smell of the air when I go back inside. I'm standing out there when I see Fred's car coming down the street. Shit!

I run back in, rushing to close doors and windows and blow out candles. I snuff the last one just as Fred walks in. I hear his footsteps pause, and he mutters, "Phew! What a reek."

He makes his way to the kitchen where I'm filling a pot with water for macaroni. "Kit? What's up with the stench in here?"

I focus on the water and shrug. "Burnt grilled cheese."

"I've burned grilled cheese before and it never smelled this bad. Mom's going to throw a hissy. Maybe we better open some windows." We race around the house, competing to see who can open the most. By the time we're done, we're laughing. I look at my brother, and an ache so fierce and deep attacks my chest that I gasp.

"Whoa, bro. You still sick or just in really bad shape?"

I shake my head and start walking away.

"Kit? Hey. I'm not trying to hassle you. Will you look at me for a minute?"

I don't.

"C'mon. What's with you? It's like your spark just goes out, man. Poof."

I don't answer him. I don't know why he's attacking me. I didn't do anything wrong. Fred's like Mom and Dad. He's on their side.

NINE

Mom gets me after dinner. She asks me to help with the dishes, and when she thinks I don't suspect anything, she starts talking. "I'm glad you're feeling better now. Did you sleep most of the day?"

"Uh. Maybe."

"Maybe?" She arches a brow and looks at me. "I tried calling a couple of times this afternoon and didn't get an answer."

Figures. She was setting me up. "Oh. Yeah. Guess I did sleep for a while."

She nods. "That's good. By the way, I got an appointment for you with the doctor."

"What? Why?"

"Well, Kit, I just think it might be a good idea for you to have a checkup."

"A checkup?"

"Yes. Please don't look at me like that."

"Like what?"

She sighs. "Never mind. Your appointment is for next Tuesday, after school. I've arranged to leave work early so I can go with you. Then maybe we can go out for coffee or something. Just the two of us. Okay?"

Not okay. The buzz in my head is back, and this time it's warning me about her. She's up to something. "I don't need to see a doctor. I'm fine."

"I hope so, Kit. But I've been thinking..." Her voice trails off and I can feel her looking at me, like she's being careful, trying not to slip up. I watch her from the corner of my eye and wait.

"It's just that I was talking to a friend of mine, and her daughter suffers from depression. And I was thinking that maybe you might..."

"You think *I'm* depressed? As if."

"But, Kit, you're not yourself. And perhaps some counseling or even medication would help. It's nothing to be ashamed of."

So that's it. She wants to drug me.

She goes on. "I don't know for sure, but it can't hurt to at least talk to the doctor, right?"

"Wrong."

"Kit, please."

"You think I'm crazy?"

"No. Of course not. That's not what I'm saying at all. It's just that you seem so unsettled. Sort of... disconnected. I've done some reading, and depression is very common in teenagers. Why should you suffer if there's help available?"

"I don't need your help."

She stops then and rests her elbows on the counter, her head in her hands. Takes a deep breath. Another. Then she drops her hands, straightens and turns toward me. "For me then, Kit?" she asks softly. "Just go, for my peace of mind? Please?"

I feel confused. I know she's plotting something and I can't trust her. But I can't say no to her either. She's the one who needs to see the doctor. Maybe I should tell her I'll go, and when we get there, I can explain to him. But next Tuesday? When is that? I try to remember what day it is now.

"Isn't today Tuesday?" I ask.

She blinks. "Yes. But I couldn't get an appointment outside school hours until *next* Tuesday."

It's simple. I'll tell her I'll go, get her off my case. By next Tuesday, I won't be here. I nod. "Okay."

She smiles and her whole face changes. The lines across her brow slip down and curve around her mouth. I wonder how she does that. It doesn't matter. I have a deadline now. I need to get everything ready. I need that charger for the Blackberry.

"Mom?"

"Yes?"

"Would it be okay if I took the car to the drug-store? I need to get something for school."

She squints at me. "You sure you're feeling well enough to go out?"

I nod.

"Maybe I should go with you."

"Jeez, Mom. It's just the store. I'll be back in half an hour."

She hesitates for another second, then nods. "Fine. The keys are on the hook. And, Kit?"

"Yeah?"

"Thank you."

"For what?"

"For agreeing to see the doctor."

"No problem." I go to the drugstore and head straight for the electronics department. Sure enough, they carry a universal charging unit for Blackberries. I find it hanging on a rack in one of those plastic bubble packages. It's only thirty dollars. I grab it and then decide I should get a few other things too. I pick up samples of junk food, including gum, a chocolate bar and chips. The chip bag has a *Best before* date on it. This strikes me as funny, but I don't stop to think about why. I get a paperback best-seller, a map book of North American roads, and a half-price calendar. I head for the checkout and then remember I need condoms too. I bought them once before, seems like a lifetime ago, when I was hoping things might go that way with Melissa.

With her, life was perfect. Everywhere we went— movies, biking, out to eat—was lit up just by her being there. I think we were invited to every party last summer, spent whole days at the beach, went on every ride when the fair came to town. It seemed like everyone was always laughing, bubbling with good times. Melissa got along great with my group of friends, and when the inevitable dramas happened, like when Joel had a big blowup with his girlfriend, both of them came to me and Melissa to talk about it. Ben gave me a hard time once in a while about us not hanging out so much, but he worked part-time at the golf course with me, and we had some good times there too.

Melissa said it was the best summer ever. And when it was just the two of us walking home, her body curled close to mine, kissing me, sighing my name, soft and low...

"You all right, kid?"

I blink back into the fluorescent glare of the drugstore and find a guy eyeballing me.

"Huh?"

"Looked like you were having a seizure or something." He glances at my hand and grins. "First time buying those?"

I look at my hand too and find it clutching a package of condoms. I don't say a word to the guy. I turn away, walk to the checkout, hand over the cash, take my bag and go home.

When I get into my room, I plug in the charger at the outlet behind my desk and stash the other stuff under my bed. I peek behind my desk and watch the red light on the charging unit, visualizing the electricity flowing into the Blackberry's lithium battery, and it's as if the energy is pumping into me too. I feel great. It's actually happening. Everything is falling into place. I go to my computer and start downloading songs. I get the seventies, the eighties, the nineties. I get the top songs since Y2K, and when that's all done, the green light is lit on the Blackberry.

Dad sticks his head in my bedroom door and says, "You still up?"

I shrug. "Just about done."

He frowns. "Hope so. Time for bed, eh?"

I nod.

I make a show of using the bathroom, splash water around, brush my teeth, flush the toilet. I get back into my room, sit down at my computer and open up my manifesto document.

<u>Category Three: Work</u>

Most people must work at jobs to earn money so they can buy things like food and clothing. They also need to pay for a place to live. If they earn enough Money, they can buy a house or an apartment, but they usually have to borrow money to do that, and it takes a long time to pay back the loan. Lots of other people rent a place to live from a wealthier person who owns extra places. Some people don't work and can end up living on the streets. Who knows why they don't work. Maybe they're sick or crazy or drug addicts or they just don't want to and they like the freedom to wander around.

I should discuss drug addicts. You will find samples of two common illegal drugs among my artifacts. The plant is marijuana which people smoke to get high. It's not supposed to be extremely harmful quite a few kids I know have tried it and they seem okay after I even tried it once. The lumps of crystal are called meth which is short for.........is supposed to make you feel really great for a short time. It is highly addictive and screws up your brain.

There is a third drug at the scene, alcohol. People get addicted to this too. It comes in many flavors and is in liquid form when you analyze my body, you should find that I drank a type of alcohol known as vodka. That's the plan. I don't usually drink this but it has the effect of numbing the senses, I will not notice myself freezing to death.

This doesn't have much to do with work, does it? There's all sorts of work. My father is a plumber he installs pipes in buildings to carry fresh water in and dirty water out. How is your water situation? I hope you're not down to drinking recycled urine. My mother's work involves a lot of paper and trying to sort out whether someone has broken the law or how people might solve legal disputes. Other people work as doctors, teachers, cooks, garbage collectors.

I wonder if you have the technology to clone me and bring me back to life. Then I could tell you in person all about life today but would my clone have my memories? Are my memories in my cells? Speaking of cells I used to have a friend whose mother was a type of massage therapist and did treatments called the Rosen Method. She told me about it. When people are injured and pretend it wasn't frightening or didn't hurt, the bodies hold those emotions in that area. Well, years later you may have a very bad pain somewhere and doctors can't figure out why but you go for Rosen treatment and when the practitioner contacts that spot the muscles clench and quiver. So the practitioner probes that place and suddenly you're crying or angry and all these horrible feelings that you suppressed start coming out this is supposed to be good because if you allow the emotions to happen, they'll be released from your flesh.

So maybe you *can* find my memories in my clone?

Category Four: Aliens

I'm pretty sure that by now you'll know if there's life on other planets lots of people claim to see UFOs

Unidentified Flying Objects (my grandfather saw one) and some people even say they've been abducted by aliens. These aliens examine the people then let them go sort of like how we catch wild animals and examine then release them.

Did I mention animals don't have it too good here sometimes? Some people are cruel to them and others use them to test chemicals and drugs it is disgusting. Hopefully by now you people won't be doing this anymore. I really hope so.

If we do get visitors from other planets I hope they're not only advanced in technology but also in ethics they will do the right thing and act kindly, maybe help us out instead of wipe us out. Of course they could be like the guys on *Star Trek* and follow the Prime Directive which would mean they couldn't interfere with our evolution.

Speaking of evolution it took a long time for my eyeteeth to come in. I had to go to an orthodontist and get braces on my teeth and he told me that some people today no longer get eyeteeth at all this could be due to evolution since humans are no longer using their teeth the way we once did—that is, we're not biting and chewing at lots of tough meat and hide which sounds pretty bad, eh? Some people don't get wisdom teeth either and those of us who do get them end up getting them pulled out. Mostly crummy molars at the back of our mouths and I should tell you when you examine my body you won't find mine there although I did have them.

My manifesto is going great. Just a few more categories to go, but I'm too tired to keep writing. The clock says it's 3:15, and that's AM for sure. I have to go to school tomorrow. Need to get the meth and weed. I'm getting close.

I crawl into bed, but even though I'm exhausted, I don't fall asleep. I lie there for a long time before I eventually drift into a strange place of half waking, half sleeping....

TEN

I'm in a canoe, casting my fishing line into an indigo alpine lake. Dark forest grows thick from the water's edge on every side, the green rising up around me in a ruffled mass. Above this is the sharp white peak of a young mountain. The mountain is close, so close I feel I could cast my line up and it would snag the peak, forming a slender connection I could swing upon and shimmy straight to the top.

But not yet. I'm utterly content here in the boat, watching sunlight wink on wavelets, peering deep into the water, glimpsing flickers of pink and green on the swift flanks of rainbow trout. I love this place. I live for such moments. And I've made it so this moment can go on for as long as I choose.

I've seen the signs of global warming in my travels around the planet; my trip to the thawing Arctic last year was the catalyst that drove me to perfect the program. Day and night, for weeks, for months, I stayed away from my love and built the solution. I sigh and lean back, trail my hand in the water, picture that building I've left behind. It's filled with computers all bent toward a single purpose: identify, beyond any doubt, the factors creating climate change.

The computers will find the proof. They are capable of seeking out all other computers, of accessing, corre-lating and analyzing all data. And since there is no more time to waste in discussion, in presenting the proof, no time at all, I programmed them to go one step further. My final instruction to them was, once the sources of the problem are discovered, be they cars, industry, jet planes—whatever—to go right ahead and activate the robots to eliminate the problems by any means necessary.

By the time I get back to civilization, things will be underway, maybe even fully implemented. Perfect. I know people will moan and gripe about the massive changes to our lifestyle, but we'll adapt. Humans are good at that. After all, we got along for millennia without burning fossil fuels or putting every little damn thing in plastic, didn't we? Yes, we must make some serious changes, and the computers will see that it's done efficiently. No more schizo waffling on what we humans must do, or undo.

We humans...I leap to my feet and, in an instant, am toppled into the water. I gasp and thrash in the icy cold and can't tell if I'm numbed by this chill or by the realization of my terrible error. The computers were instructed to eliminate the problem. But if the ultimate problem is us...! I struggle to reach the canoe. I must get back, must shut them down, stop them...

"Kit? Hey! You're having a bad dream. Kit?"

From far away, I hear myself screaming, "Stop them! Must stop them!"

And again, the soft voice, urgently calling. "Kit? Come on, wake up. It's okay. Just a nightmare."

I'm not drowning in a distant lake. I'm tangled in the blankets on my bed, coated in a film of cold sweat, gasping. My heart is pounding so hard it feels as though it's trying to burst from my chest. Mom is leaning over me. Dad too.

"Kit?"

I croak, "Yeah."

"Wow. Must have been some nightmare. You were screaming, honey. Are you okay?"

I sink back against my pillow and manage a nod.

"I'm going to get a damp cloth and some water, okay? I'll be right back." Mom's anxious face disappears from my line of vision, and Dad's takes its place.

"Must have been a doozy, kid. Haven't heard you have a nightmare like that for years. Scared the bejeesus out of me."

"Sorry."

He shakes his head. "No, no need to apologize. Can't be helped. Do you want to talk about it?"

I can't tell him what I did. It still feels so real. I, Kit Latimer, single-handedly caused the annihilation of humanity and the rise of the machine. How could I have been so colossally stupid? I shudder, and Dad pats my arm.

"Never mind. Maybe later. Here's Mom back."

And there she is, patting a cool cloth over my face, just like she did when I was a little kid. She finishes and offers a glass of water. "Drink?"

I take the glass and swallow. The water going down my dry throat feels icy cold. I hand back the glass and mutter, "Thanks."

She straightens out my bedding and says, "Would you like me to sit with you for a bit?"

I shake my head.

She purses her lips and nods. "Okay. Maybe we can all catch one more hour of sleep, eh?"

I glance at the clock and see that it's almost 6:00 AM. One more hour until it's time to get up, go off to school, off to score. I nod and wait for her to leave the room; then I throw off my blankets and get up. No way am I risking going back into that nightmare. I sit at my desk and watch the minutes tick by on my clock. They tick in unison with my heartbeat.

This small machine is in tune with my body. I reach around and feel my tattoo. Tattoo. That's a word that can also mean a beat or a rhythm, isn't it? I keep a hand on my back and my eyes on the clock and sure enough, it's all synchronized. What does it mean?

There's a pattern here, I'm sure of it. The machines in the dream, my heart beating a tattoo in sync with my clock, in sync with my tattoo…A chill runs through me as I realize that some of the nanos must have survived. They've made it to my heart, haven't they? But so what? They can't do anything. There aren't enough of them. Maybe only two or three, the size of bacteria. That's the message of my night-mare. It must be. The nanos have survived and are on the move.

A glimmer of another dream I had recently surfaces. It was about the nanos, wasn't it? Do computers make nanos? Now that I think about it, how could people make something that small? It's impossible. I switch on my computer and type in a search for nanos. Thousands of hits come up and I start clicking. Sure enough, to be effective, the nano robots must exist in swarms. But then I learn that the objective of some scientists is to make them self-replicating. The web page I read says this is still theo-retical, but is it? They don't want us to know what they're really doing, do they? What if they've already made the self-replicating nanos and are keeping the technology a secret?

I should report Tony. It's the right thing to do. How many unsuspecting people have gone into his parlor for tattoos and come out with a whole lot more than they bargained for? What if there are thousands of people being injected all over the planet, and when the time comes, the nanos are signaled to self-replicate and take over the bodies they're in?

I stand and start pacing. I need to think this through. I could go to the police and tell them, but I'll bet they won't believe me. Could I tell Fred? No, he wouldn't believe me either. Nobody wants to believe such things are happening in the world. Maybe I could write a letter to someone? Who? Man, it's so bizarre this is happening when I should be focusing on my own special mission. I can't delay my mission. But I can't go and leave this unreported either. It's bad enough I stole the Blackberry, never mind turning my back on everyone for the sake of the people in the future. If the nanos take over now, there might not even *be* people in the future.

I should write to the government. But what if they're in on it? I'll bet Tony is an agent for the government, a front man posing as a tattooist. But would everyone in the government be in on it? So maybe I'll write to lots of governments and the United Nations and all the churches because for sure they would think it's evil for machines to take over humans.

The faint buzz of my parents' alarm startles me. When I look at my clock, I find the whole hour has gone by already. Ike was definitely right about time speeding up.

. . . .

Another buzz. This time it signals the end of English class, and I automatically gather my books and rise to my feet.

"Kit Latimer? I'd like to speak with you for a moment. Please remain seated." Mr. Porter doesn't sound happy.

I slump back into my desk.

Mr. Porter waits until the other students have exited, going off to eat their lunches. I'm supposed to be on my way to get my weed and meth, so whatever he has to say, I hope he gets it over with fast.

He approaches me and sits at the desk next to mine. I don't look at him, but I can feel him staring, willing me to meet his gaze. It's an old teachers' trick, and I'm immune. He says, "I know what you're thinking."

And with horrifying certainty, I realize this is true. He knows. He knows everything. He knows about the nanos. I don't look at him. I can't let him see that I understand or, worse yet, allow him access to my eyes. He'd have total control then, wouldn't he?

"Kit?"

I shake my head.

He sighs. "You think if you ignore me, then maybe I'll just do the same, right? But I can't do that, Kit. It's my job to teach, and it gives me a great deal of satisfaction. The thing is, it's a two-way street. In order for me to teach, I need my students to learn. Have you learned anything at all in this class?"

It's a trick question. He wants to know what I know. I shrug.

Another sigh. "Listen, Kit. I looked at your records. Up until this year, you were a good student. Very good. But we're several weeks into the new semester, and you haven't yet handed in a single assignment."

I keep quiet.

"I also give marks for class participation, but I don't recall you contributing to any class discussions. I've got to tell you, Kit, I'm concerned about your chances for passing this course—one that's required for graduation. You do understand this, don't you?"

I force a nod. I understand all right.

"Good. What I'd like to suggest is that, for the next while, you spend the lunch hour in my classroom. Just until you're caught up. I'm going to write a letter explaining this to your parents, all right?

I'll have it ready for you tomorrow, and then I need it returned to me, with their signatures, by Friday."

He's planning to get my parents in on it. I feel sick.

"Kit?"

I keep my eyes glued to the top of the desk.

"Are you okay? Maybe you should meet with the counselor too. I can speak to Mrs. Jamieson if you like."

"No, thanks."

"No? Hmm. Well, we'll see how it goes with the extra class time first, but if I don't see any improvement...Look, is there anything you'd like to tell me?"

Like I'm going to fall for that.

"Okay, then. Go ahead and have your lunch. I'll have the letter ready for tomorrow. Understood?"

I nod, get to my feet and go. There is no way I can ever go back into that classroom. No way at all. I shuffle down the hallway; it's almost deserted. Almost. A group of guys hangs in a knot on one side. Farther down, two girls sit on the floor, their backs against the wall. All of them stare at me. The guys huddle closer and murmur; the girls incline their heads together and whisper. They're all talking about me. I'll bet if they were naked I could see their tattoos. They've been taken. They're waiting for me to be taken too.

I force myself to walk past them, even though I have the overpowering urge to run. Or scream, tell them I know all about their plans. Why me? I'd like to ask them that. I hesitate. Maybe I should ask them. Maybe there's some shred of humanity left in one of them and they'll help me escape.

No. I don't need their help. It's too big a risk, like handing myself on a platter to a pack of soul-sucking zombies. I make it past them and speed up, go straight for my locker. I'm going to empty it, take everything I own and go. I'll have to make sure I get every last bit of me, even a stray hair that may have fallen; I can take no chances of them having access to my DNA. No chances.

ELEVEN

My laden backpack feels unnaturally heavy, as though the books are super-weighted, but if something has been planted in them, the discovery will have to wait until later. First things first. And the first thing now is getting the last thing I need from this so-called school.

The kids hanging in the clearing watch me plod into their midst with the barest flicker of interest. These ones have not been taken by the nanos; not yet, anyway. They've been taken by the drugs. The pungent odor of weed drifts on the air, along with their lazy chuckles, and I approach the first knot of stoners with something like relief.

I say, "Hey."

"Kit?"

It's only then that I notice the girl I'm standing next to is Melissa. I stare at her, uncomprehending. How can she be here?

"Kit? What's up?"

Someone else says, "You know this guy?"

"I used to," she says.

"Melissa," I say. "Hi." I fix my gaze on her face, and it's like a magnet finding metal. There's an actual force, irresistibly pulling me into the field of her being.

She blinks and exhales a fluttery little laugh. "So. Got some studying to do?"

A few more chuckles circle the group, and I say, "What do you mean?"

"Um, your backpack, Kit. Looks like you've got half the library stuffed in there."

"Oh. That. Never mind. Do you know who deals weed and meth around here?"

She shakes her head. "What?"

"I'd like to buy some."

She takes hold of my arm and pulls me aside. "Kit," she whispers, "what's the matter with you?"

Her touch is amazing. Electricity zings through my arm, fires nerve endings, arcs straight into my heart. It's unbelievable, as though her touch alone has sparked a circuit that could neutralize the nanos,

121

melt them into nothing. "Wow," I breathe.
come with me?"

"What? Where?"

"To the mountain."

She shakes her head. "Something's wr[...]
you, man." Her hand drops away and her eye[...]
"Are you really into this stuff now, Kit?"

The withdrawal of her touch leaves me c[...]
weary. "No. Well, yes, sort of. I just need s[...]
an…experiment."

Her brow wrinkles and she gnaws on her[...]
lip. I used to kiss that lip. I lean forward and
my mouth across hers.

She steps back. "What did you do that for?"

I shrug.

She folds her arms across her chest and l[...]
around to see if anyone has noticed me kiss her.
she looks back at me. "I think you should go."

"I will. But I need the stuff."

"Fine. Whatever. It's none of my business, i[...]
See that guy over there in the black jacket?" [...]
points.

"Yeah."

"Ask him. He usually has everything."

"Will he sell to me?"

I can't tell if the thick fog of [...]
the air is coming from her or me.

. . . .

I empty my backpack when I g[...]
everything under my bed. Now w[...]
my manifesto.

Category Five: Religion

I'm not a religious person I don't g[...]
I did go to Sunday school for a [...]
a higher power which most pe[...]
people don't believe in God bec[...]
fairy tale or wishful thinking or [...]
as I can see life is mystery there'[...]
bigger than us. if the universe st[...]
what made it go boom?

We studied religion in Socia[...]
some documentaries about it to [...]
three main Western religions wh[...]
and Muslims. I don't know why [...]
because they all started in an[...]

The Middle East and all of them say Jerusalem is their Holy City and they fight over it. Go figure. There are other religions too, like Hinduism and Buddhism and stuff, plus there are Pagans which I think are people who believe the planet Earth is alive and it's called Gaia. All religions believe there's something bigger than puny people but they argue about who is right. they all got together one time to see what they agreed on. Here's what they came up with: *Do unto others as you'd have them do unto you*. the Golden Rule if they all believe in it, then why don't they follow it? people go to war about religion and blow each other up, but do they want someone to do that to them???? I don't think so.

I hope by the time you read this people will have just one religion and that will be that. Or none. Possibly aliens will attack and fix this. maybe the only way the people of our planet will unite is if they're attacked by an outside force that makes us look pretty stupid, doesn't it?

In Hinduism they believe that people get reincarnated and if they're right then I'll back here soon in a different body in which case cloning me and getting my Mind back wouldn't work would it!!! Is the mind the same as the soul? Maybe not. I think only the soul comes back and where you end up has something to do with your Karma. If you did something bad during this lifetime that would give bad Karma and it would stick with you into the next life until you balanced it by doing something good. This is why there's a caste system in India. I wonder why more people don't do real work as in grow food and make things? And spend more time together Most people in India are Hindus and it's the oldest religion on the planet and they figure if you were crummy person last time around you'll be born back into the low caste which is the Untouchables. These people are treated badly and live in extreme poverty but other Hindus there don't really feel sorry for them since they figure they deserve what they got and things will be better in the next lifetime. Also, the cow is sacred in India so when people say, "Holy Cow!" that's why. The only holy book I've got with me is the bible. Jews and Christians use it. Muslims use the Koran. One last thing on this category I know some religious people think if you kill yourself that's very bad Karma or you will go to hell I'm not really killing myself I'm preserving myself Right?

I can't keep writing. There's plenty more for me to do, but I need to gather my thoughts. I sit on the bed and

I guess I doze off because the next thing I know, Fred is standing beside me.

"You still sick, man?"

I rub my eyes and consider this. Was I sick? Yes, I had a stomach bug and now my body feels like sand runs in my veins; it's far too heavy to move it from the bed. I nod.

"That's too bad. I thought maybe we'd go out somewhere. Get a burger or something."

I shake my head.

He sits down at my desk, tilts the chair back and locks his hands behind his neck. What does he want?

"Seen any good movies lately?" he asks.

"No."

"I saw one the other day. It was pretty good. Sci-fi, lots of action. You'd like it."

"Yeah?"

"For sure." He glances at me, then asks, "How did your mountain report go? Get a good mark?"

"What?"

"You told me you had to write about snow on the mountains or your experience or something."

"Why are you asking me this?"

He shrugs. "No special reason. Just thought we could talk a bit. You want to help me out with that?"

"What do you mean?"

"I mean, tell me something. What's new? What's happening? Whatever."

"There's nothing to tell."

"No? Come on, there must be something. Hey, you remember when you were going to build a boat? I was thinking, maybe we could work on that together. It's almost spring, and if we got the plans ready now, we could probably start building it soon. What do you think?"

"I don't want to build a boat anymore."

"Why not? It'd be cool. We make the boat, and then we could go fishing, right? Didn't you want to make one of those old-school canoes out of cedar or something?"

My nightmare explodes in my mind, and goose bumps ripple over my skin. I stare at Fred. He knows about it? How?

"Kit? What's wrong, dude?"

"How do you know about that?" I ask.

"About what? The canoe? You told me about it, remember?"

I didn't tell him about it. I know I didn't.

"So what do you say? You want to try it?"

"No."

"Why not?"

"Why are you hassling me?"

Fred drops his hands and leans forward. "I'm not trying to hassle you, Kit. I'm just trying to...Man, I don't know! I'm just trying to talk to you, okay? What's up with you anyway?"

"I won't be here." Shit! Shit! I said that out loud? Did I?

"What do you mean you won't be here?"

I did say it out loud. I am so stupid. Think, Kit. Think. "I mean I won't be here because...I'm thinking of going traveling. For the summer."

He grins. "Really? That's awesome. Who's going with you?"

"Ike."

Fred says, "Yeah? Don't think I've met him. What about Ben? Is he going too?"

"Maybe."

"Good stuff, man. So what's it going to be, a backpacking trek or a road trip? Where are you guys going?"

I shrug. "We haven't decided for sure. Maybe backpacking."

"That's cool. Have you told Mom and Dad yet?"

"Nope."

"Well, just in case they think it's a bad idea, let me give you some advice. If I were you, I'd mention it soon so you've got a few months to work on them."

I don't have a few months to work on anything, but I don't say this out loud. I only say, "Good idea."

Fred nods. "You want me to be there when you tell them? Back you up?"

"Sure."

"Excellent." He looks as if he wants to say something more but doesn't know what. He starts whistling and tapping his fingers on my desk. Then his hand bumps the mouse and the screen flashes awake, displaying a web page on nanotechnology. He starts reading.

"Screw off," I say.

He startles and turns to me, frowning. "What?"

"I don't like people looking at my stuff."

He blinks. "Dude. It's a website. What's the big deal?"

"It's on my computer."

He holds up both hands, palms out. "Sorry. Didn't know it meant so much to you."

"It does. And it's none of your business."

He sighs. "Yeah? You know, you actually used to like me. Remember that?"

This is confusing. It's as if we were playing basketball and then somehow we're suddenly playing chess. I can't think of anything to say to him.

Fred gets to his feet. "Whatever. You know, maybe you'd feel better if you had a shower. You look like hell, and you don't smell too good either. Catch you later." And he goes.

I lie back on my bed and try to figure out what's going on with everybody. I can't. Or maybe I just don't want to face the fact that the entire world is screwed up, and the reason I have to go on my mission is so that one normal human will be preserved for the future.

The enormity of this realization washes over me in cold waves. It's down to just me, Kit Latimer. Maybe Ike too, but that's another thing; I haven't heard from Ike since the day we took the Blackberry. Maybe he was caught and I'm on my own.

It's too much. I can't do it. Only maybe it's like Frodo in *The Lord of the Rings*. He didn't want to be a ring bearer, but it was his appointed task and he had to do it. I have to do this.

I haul myself off my bed and sit at the computer. I pull up my artifact list and skim through it. The only things still possible for me to buy are more books and the solar energy panel. Do I need more books? I don't. Do I need the solar energy panel? I can't even remember why we had that on the list. Something to do with powering the laptop computer, which I'm not getting anyway? Must have been that. So I don't need it either. Which means all I have left to do is transfer the music onto the Blackberry, shoot a one-minute video of myself, finish writing the manifesto and pack everything onto the sled.

TWELVE

It's late when Ike shows up, almost midnight. I've finished transferring the music and am about to get going on completing my manifesto when suddenly there he is.

"Are you ready, man?"

"Jeez, Ike. You scared me. How did you get in?"

He sniggers. "I have my ways. I saw your light on, so here I am."

I keep my voice low—I don't want to risk waking anyone. "Where have you been?"

"Around. So are you ready to go?"

"Now?"

"Hell, yes. Now."

"Um, almost. Just need to finish the manifesto and pack up."

"You haven't finished that friggin' thing yet? Shit, you writing a novel or what? Trust me, dude, you don't have that much great stuff to say."

"I've been sick, okay? But I got the weed and the meth and the condoms. Got the music on the…"

"Did I say I wanted every single stupid detail? Have you got a map?"

"Yeah, I got a map book of the roads in North America, plus I downloaded some world maps and stored them on my computer. And I put on a bunch of Wikipedia articles and saved some Google Earth satellite shots too." Ike is making a snoring sound, so I stop.

"You done?" he asks. When I keep quiet, he says, "Thank you. The map I was talking about was one of Strathcona Park. You think you're just going to drive up to the perfect spot, park and, *poof*, there you are?"

Damn. He's right. I'm familiar with some of the trails in the park, but I'm going to need to know which one to follow for the ice mountain. Can't believe I didn't think of that.

"As usual, you're not thinking, doofus. You've got to plan ahead, don't you?"

In reply, I type in a search, and within seconds I have several hits for the park. I click on a link and, *bam*, there's a file for trails. I click on that and I've got a map. "Satisfied?" I ask.

"So, you going to print it or do you intend to memorize it?"

"I can't print it now. It'll make too much noise."

"So in other words, we can't go now, right? Figures."

"I thought we'd go Friday night. That way, Mom won't be stuck without her car to go to work the next day."

"You're so considerate, Kit. Your mommy's going to be so happy with you."

"Shut up," I hiss. "Besides, everyone usually sleeps in on Saturday. If we go after they're in bed on Friday night, we'll be long gone before they suspect a thing."

"You think? Whatever. Okay, what day is this? Thursday? We can go tomorrow night?"

I try to remember what day it is, but I can't be sure.

Ike repeats his question. "We're going tomorrow night?"

"Yes. Tomorrow night."

"Fine. You be ready then. No more bullshit whining about this or that not being done. You promise?"

"For sure."

Ike chuckles, soft and low. "Awesome, man. I'll see you tomorrow night then." And he goes.

It's only after he's gone that I realize tomorrow is only Thursday. It must be because I was supposed to go to school and get that letter from Mr. Porter. As if. Well, too late now. Guess Mom will just have to take the bus to work on Friday morning. No biggie.

I minimize the map of the park and bring up the document for my manifesto.

Category Six: Science

Science today is mainly divided into biology chemistry physics some things just don't fit neatly into those slots and there's some overlapping too For example when a plant goes through photosynthesis I'd say that's a mix of biology and chemistry. Okay that's quite boring I guess i want to say that I like science and find it quite interesting although its bad when science makes things like nuclear bombs and manufactures anti-matter at secret laboratories places like CERN in Switzerland. Speaking of Matter this is what we currently know about the universe. Almost nothing Scientists estimate that only 4% of the universe is made up of the sort of matter known to us a lousy 4%. They call this known type of Matter baryons. They figure that 73% of the universe is something called Dark Energy and 23% is Dark Matter And get this They don't know what dark energy and dark Matter really *is* All they know is that dark matter is cold and it's invisible that seems hilarious like they're trying to impress us saying there's this invisible stuff they know about. Turns out they do know something is there because light rays coming from distant galaxies bend around the dark matter like light bends through the eye glasses.

Still wearing eyeglasses? Plus they launched a space telescope called Chandra and since its clear of the earth's atmosphere it can see things like x-rays. X-ray vision just like Superman I would like to be SuperMan BatMan. SpiderMan. Hero. what do x-rays have to do with the dark Matter? can't remember If I were smart enough I'd like to solve the mystery of dark matter. The conspiracy people know It's supposed to be out there in massive patches like clouds or enormous banks of fog But it seems impossible to understand something

that is so unlike us We even have trouble understanding ourselves never mind thing like that Maybe
you're having a laugh now because dark Matter is old
news and all understood. But I wonder...ever figured
us out?

I'm tired. The clock says it's 2:00 AM, but I still have a
lot to do. I better keep going. Just one more category
to write. Only, if I'm not going to school anymore,
I can finish everything during the day tomorrow,
can't I?

I crawl into bed, lie back, close my eyes. I can't
sleep. I feel like I've forgotten something important.
Thoughts fly through my mind, swift and erratic as
leaves on the wind. Melissa. Music. Manifesto. Map.
Mountain. I realize that all of those things start with
the letter *M*. Why am I stuck on *M*? More *M* words
start skittering into my mind: motion, muscle, magic,
magnificent, moan, mirth, meet. I can't seem to stop
them. Measles, mouth, modern, mitten, moon. The
*M*s are taking control of my mind. My mind. Me.
Myself. More *M*s!

I leap from my bed and pace. There has to be
a way to stop this. What letter comes after *M*?

In a flash, I have it. *N.* Yes, it's *N.* For nano. It's them again, trying to block me from seeing their nasty work. Nasty, night, nincompoop. Terminano. I've got it now. The terminanos are on the move. *Snap!* That's what I forgot. The letter to the governments. The warning. I must write the warning.

To Whom Concern:
Leaders of the **Planet Earth**

I Must warn that world in great danger!!!!!!!!!!!! All persons who have tattooed have been injected with nano robots which programmed to take control their host bodies. I don't know who or what is behind this plot but you act swiftly to put a stop to this!!!!!!!!!!!!!!!!! I self was injected with nanos called Terminanos when tattoo at **Tony's Tattoo** parlor in Nanaimo but Managed detect their presence quickly to neutralize the swarM. While still some renegade **terminanos** on loose in body their numbers few to control me entirely I dead very soon due to primary Mission but not leave without telling you this first Good luck

~~Kit Latimer~~

I read over the letter and wonder if I should add more in the way of evidence, but I think I've covered the main points. I don't have time to print and mail a bunch of paper copies so I start surfing the net for contacts on government websites. I e-mail Canada first, then the USA, Russia, England, India, Australia...Suddenly the task seems over-whelming. I can't e-mail every country in the world, not in the time I have. So I send a copy to the High Commissioner for Human Rights at the United Nations. Another to the Pope in Rome, then one to the Dalai Lama. Then my mind just goes blank. I'm exhausted. I can do no more.

ThirTEEN

When Mom tries to get me up for school, I can't even respond. I just can't. After a while she gives up and goes away, and I go back to sleep. It's early afternoon by the time I wake up, and that's only because I need to pee and I need to eat. I do both and feel way better, until I realize that I just ate one of my last meals. Peanut butter on toast, a banana, a chunk of cheese and about ten chocolate chip cookies with a tall glass of milk.

Was this a good choice? Is this a typical meal? How should I know? I can imagine what Ike would say. He'd say I should have researched this, got some statistics to work with so I'd know. Too late now.

I go to my room and start packing. Baseball hat, check. Card collection in Baggie, check. Junk food, check. Condoms, check. Weed and meth, check. Seashell fossils, check. Lego, check. Map book and Bible, check. I stuff in a couple of textbooks—geography and biology—then try to decide what to put in next. The vodka! I grab that out of the closet and put it in my backpack. I haul out the clothes I'll need too: winter coat, gloves, tuque, hiking boots. I don't know if my boots will work for walking on ice, but they'll have to do.

The thought of walking on ice reminds me: I need to print the map of the trails in the park. The first printing goes goofy, with a squiggle through the middle, but the second one is perfect and I fold it carefully, tuck it into a pocket on my pack. I look around. All that's left is the Blackberry and my computer. I need to make the video for the Blackberry, but it feels stupid to do that by myself. Maybe I'll wait and do it on the mountain with Ike. Yeah, for sure, that'll be better. I stuff the Blackberry in my pack too and now...

What was that noise? Someone just came into the house. I heard the door. Ike? No, he said he'd come

tonight. Maybe Fred? I scramble to hide the pack and
the clothes in my closet, then I carefully open my
bedroom door. What if one of the governments has
tracked my e-mail and sent a representative to talk to
me? Could it happen that fast? I think it could.

Cupboard doors bang in the kitchen, pots clatter,
cutlery rattles. Mom? Damn. It's that late already?
I take a deep breath. It's okay. I'm ready. The only
thing left to do is the manifesto, and I can do that
after supper. I take another breath and notice something. Fred was right. I smell bad. It's not that long
since I showered, is it?

I take a shower and when I come out, I feel great.
I'm ready. I go downstairs and find Mom, Dad and
Fred all hanging out in the kitchen. They stop talking
and stare at me.

"What?" I ask.

Nobody says anything for a minute, and then
Mom says, "Are you feeling better?"

I nod.

"Good. That's good, Kit."

Fred makes a show of sniffing the air and says,
"He smells better too. Is that my cologne?"

He doesn't sound mad, so I nod again.

He grins. "Yeah? Maybe I know why you want to smell good. Maybe something to do with a certain girl?"

Dad looks up. "A girl? You got a girlfriend, Kit?"

"I don't know what he's talking about," I say.

"No?" Fred rolls his eyes. "I happened to run into Melissa today, at the store. She said she was hanging out with you yesterday."

My stomach does a flip, and I step toward Fred. "What did she say?"

"Whoa, easy, dude. Is it supposed to be top secret or what?"

I look straight at him and can't tell if his grin means he knows about the drugs or not. It seems like he knows something. I can't stand to look at him. I turn to Mom and ask, "What's for dinner?"

"Food," she says. It's one of those stupid jokes of hers. She thinks it's funny to just say food, even now, when it's so important.

"Are you seeing Melissa again?" Dad asks.

"I'm not sure that's such a great idea," Mom says.

"Why not?" Fred asks.

"Because, after the last time…" She lets it hang.

"I'M NOT SEEING HER! FRED'S FULL OF SHIT! GOD. HE MAKES ME SICK!"

Silence again.

Fred bangs his fist on the table. Leaves the room.

I wish I'd said good-bye to him.

My last meal is chicken with pasta and salad. Very typical, for my house anyway. There's store-bought carrot cake for dessert, and I eat that too. I say, "Thanks, Mom. Thanks, Dad."

They hesitate; then in unison they say, "You're welcome, Kit."

I go to my room. I open up the manifesto on my computer but no words come to me. Not good. I have to do this. I drum my fingers on my desk and wait for inspiration, but instead I think about Fred. Why did he have to see Melissa? I have this woozy sensation in my gut, a sickly sort of fear that she told him about the drug deal.

I should call her. Ask her. Once I've got that cleared up, I'll be able to write. What should I say? Just ask her flat out if she is a narc? No. That would be wrong. Don't want her to get mad at me. Mad. That's an *M* word. Oh, man. Man? I don't want to get mugged by them again. Mugged. No. I won't let it happen.

Melissa. There's more (More) to her than *M*. Think, Kit. Her phone number. I know her phone number.

The sequence flits through my mind (Mind) and I run downstairs to get the phone. I take it back to my room and tap my fingers lightly over the keys. Yes. I know the number. I called it enough times it's engraved in my memory (Memory).

I feel a growing desperation. This is so messed up (Messed). I bang my fist on my desk and the noise helps clear my thoughts. Maybe (Maybe) the sting of pain helps too. I shake out my hand and stare at the reddened skin; it reminds me of another time I slammed my fist into a wall, and I guess that was because of Melissa too, but I can't remember the details.

Melissa used to see me. Really see me. Her eyes are this incredible shade, like a blend of chocolate and amber, and when she looked at me, it was like I was the only thing she saw. It felt like I filled her vision, and that look made me so much more than I was. We went to this little café one time, the sort that plays old-school music, and this song came on, "I Only Have Eyes for You," and Melissa looked at me and smiled. She didn't say anything, she didn't have to, but I felt like she was the one singing those words for me, and I thought it would be like that forever. Her gaze on me, that rapt attention when I spoke;

the way she laughed at my lame jokes; the way she just got right inside my space, snuggled up like a kitten, close and warm.

It was as if she brought me out of myself, or maybe as if she invited herself in, I don't know. Either way, she got close. Closer than anybody. And then she took herself away. I can't blame her for that. I finally understand. She wouldn't be the girl I know she is if she chose to stay with someone like me, would she? She's way out of my league. My fingers find the keys on the phone pad, and her mom answers. I say, "Hello, could I please speak to Melissa?" and her mom says, "Just a minute, please."

And then Melissa says, "Hello?"

Heat floods through me, settles in my skin, and I croak, "Hey. It's me."

"Kit?"

"Yeah."

"Oh. Hey."

"Listen, I just had to tell you. I understand. It's all right."

"What are you talking about?" she asks.

She doesn't know? That's strange. "About us. I get it now. You were way too good for me, right? I'm glad you figured it out."

Silence. And then, "Kit, are you okay?"

"Totally. Yeah. Absolutely. I'm good."

"I don't know about that."

"Why not?"

A sigh. "Kit…This is weird, don't you think?"

"What's weird?"

"It's been, what, over three months? I just…Okay. Cool. I don't want to go there again. I'm glad that you're good. Thanks for letting me know. I'll see you around, eh?"

"Um, yeah. Sure. But, Melissa?"

"What?"

"You saw Fred today?"

"Yeah. So?"

"So you didn't, you know, say anything to him about the, uh, drugs, right?"

"Excuse me?"

"Never mind. Forget it. I know you wouldn't. It's cool. What were you doing there, anyway?"

"What's it to you?"

"Just wondered."

"I was with Chelsea. Her boyfriend smokes weed and…Whatever. Listen, I've got to go, okay?"

"Yeah," I say, "me too. Big time."

"Bye, Kit."

I can't say good-bye so I just hang up and sit there with the phone in my hand. When it rings, I'm so startled I drop it. I pick it up and find one of Mom's friends asking for her. Not Melissa? I don't say anything and a tiny distant voice from the phone starts going, "Hello? Hello?"

I click it off again, take the phone downstairs, and by the time I get there, it's ringing again. Damn! So annoying. I watch it ring until Mom comes to get it. For no reason, she gives me a strange look, and I know I have to hurry.

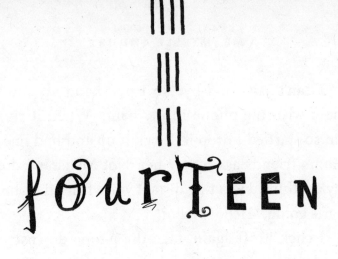

foUrTEEN

Hurry. What is it I must do? I know. Finish my manifesto, the final category.

Category Seven: Reality

I write about this because I don't think any1 knows what is reality or truth We do not know that either For exaMple if there was a car accident and five witnesses each of theM would describe it just a little differently. All of theM would think they were telling the truth but there would be differences So how can we find the truth? If two people you know get an argument and both of theM tell you it will sound like two things happened and unless you were there you wouldn't know for sure what happened. Even then you Might not There's this experiMent I heard about on the radio SoMe scientists Made a Machine that slice pennies up in randoM The pennies could split through the center or be cut in half and the scientists designed this so they could not see which slice was done by the Machine. Then they placed pennies in envelopes and Mailed to different people When those people got their envelope they called the scientists and asked What cut of the penny did I get?

The scientists said, Whatever one you think you got And there's the weird part Sure enough the recipient would think okay i got the side of the penny with a head on it and open the envelope and there it was Reality is what you expect it to be. Matter behaves differently when it is observed Can't reMeMber how they know what it's doing when they're not looking but they can tell the difference There's another experiMent They took soMe Microscopic cells out of the Mouth of a subject along with soMe saliva and put that in another rooM then had the person watch Movies that caused eMotions—happy sad angry. When people had eMotions there were tiny changes detected in the cells in the other rooM. Which is Maybe why happy people tend to get sick less often their cells are happier too. So in this experiMent they hooked a sensor to the cell/ saliva Mix in the other rooM and guess what As soon as the person experienced an eMotion there were cheM-ical changes in the cell saliva Mix in the other rooM that showed they were reacting!!!!!

Not sure what this has to do with reality but it seeMs to Me that we are More connected than we think. The air isn't eMpty is it? It's a Mixture of gases that are Made up of known particles like baryons when we Move we don't take our bodies with us Our essence siMply follows our intention then flows and reforMs into what *looks like* a solid body out of the particles we Moved into.

Also Einsteins theory of relativity which I don't really understand but I know explains soMe things about space tiMe and light. TiMe Moves More slowly on top of a Mountain or in space ship going away from earth than at sea level because the closer the clock is to the gravity source earth the More tiMe speeds up It does seeM that when we go up the Mountain tonight my tiMe will slow down which could be good because it's been speeding up and I'M not really saying what Maybe this.................reality is what we think it is

And it's different for everyone and nobody can say their reality is better than soMeone elses because how know??????????? And if a person went to heaven then their heaven just exactly what they want with the right birds and plants and Maybe their old dog We had dog naMed Harry and he shed everywhere so MoM never wanted to get another one after died and she went to work and didn't have time to clean I loved harry and get to see hiM again in My heaven which is close now and has My younger self in it because i get to choose what i coMe back as when not the tiMe of this when he never knew he couldn't do anything that he had awful destiny to freeze death alone because soMeone has to do it iMportant

It's done. I look over what I've written and it looks strange, almost like I didn't do it, but there's no time to change it. I hit the Print button and the printer spews out my manifesto. I save the document on my computer too, and then I turn it off and unplug it. I fold the manifesto carefully, put it in an envelope, then go to the kitchen and grab several plastic bags. What is it they say about plastic? It'll last forever? That's good in this case because it will keep my manifesto safe. I get one of those big plastic garbage bags too, big enough to put my whole backpack inside.

From the living room, Dad asks, "What are you doing in there, Kit?"

"Nothing. I'm going to bed now."

"Yeah? Well, good night, then."

Mom echoes him. "Good night, Kit. Hope you have a good sleep."

"Thanks," I mutter. A good sleep? I don't think so.

I wait in my room with the light off, wait for my parents to go to bed, wait longer for them to fall asleep. I listen outside their door, and sure enough, Dad is snoring, Mom too, the pair of them making a weird harmony. I go back to my room, put on all my mountain clothes, pick up my pack and creep downstairs to the kitchen. Mom's car keys are right there on the hook. I take them and go outside to the car. Put my pack in. Go into the garage and find the old sled. I put it in the car. I go back up to my room and get my computer, take it downstairs, put it in the car. I should wrap it in a few layers of plastic too. I get more garbage bags for that, and when I get back to the car, there's Ike.

"Dude. You're actually ready?"

"I am."

"Well, whaddaya know? Freakin' amazing. So let's go, eh?"

I nod. I get behind the wheel, take one last look at my house, and we're off. Within minutes we're on the highway, heading north.

"You know the way?" Ike asks.

"No problem. I've been to the park lots of times. Maybe not in the dark, but we'll notice the turnoff for Mount Washington."

"Mount Washington? We're not going skiing, you idiot."

"Did I say we were? That's just where we turn off the highway, okay?"

Ike grunts. "Yeah? Well, I'll believe it when I see it."

I switch on the radio and crank the volume. That keeps him quiet for a while. It's a short drive to the turnoff, and then we're on the Strathcona Parkway. We don't pass a single other car, and I glance down at the clock and note that it's just after one in the morning.

I turn down the radio. "Uh, Ike?"

"What?"

"It's going to be pitch-dark when we get there. Think we should just wait in the car until dawn?"

"Ah, man, I don't know. Did you bring any food?"

"Just some junk-food samples."

"Well that's retarded. What about your last meal?"

"I ate dinner."

"And you think that's going to hold you for a day of hiking? Go back."

"Go back? You want to call it off?"

"I don't mean *back* back, stupid. I mean just go to a drive-through and we'll grab a few burgers or something. Beats sitting around in a freakin' freezing car in the dark, doesn't it?"

He's got a point. I brake and turn the car around. Then I think to check the gas gauge. "We don't have enough gas to go back."

"Well, we'll just have to get some, won't we? You do have some cash, don't you?"

"Yeah. I've got some. But I thought it would be good to have that on me as another artifact."

"So we'll just put twenty bucks in the tank, get the food, and we'll be fine, right?"

It feels wrong to be going back the way we came, but burgers do sound good. We get the gas first, and when I count my money, I still have over two hundred dollars. Me and Ike can have a feast.

So we go to the drive-through and place our order. Two burgers each, large fries and large sodas too. When I pull forward to the window to pay and pick up the food, the girl looks at me and laughs. "Hungry, huh?"

I shrug and hand her a couple of twenties. When she reaches out to take it, I see her tattoo, a small rose on the inside of her wrist. "No wonder you're a freak," I mutter.

"Pardon me?"

It's not worth talking about. It's too late for her. But I feel sorry for her, and as she hands me the food and then the change, I say, "Keep it. And good luck."

Her eyes widen, but before she can say more, I press down on the gas and go.

"What'd you do that for?" Ike asks.

I stuff a handful of fries into my mouth and talk around them. "Her tattoo."

"What about it?"

I've never told Ike about the terminanos. Should I tell him? No. There's no point in getting him worked up about that. "Never mind," I mutter. And I crank up the radio and get back on the highway.

We turn onto the Parkway again, and when I take a certain curve in the road, it's like a curve back in time. Last summer, Dad wanted to take Fred and me back-country camping for the weekend, get in some "just us guys" time. We were in Dad's SUV, cruising with the oldies channel, singing (if you could call it that) along with Dylan's "Like a Rolling Stone."

There were some deer on the road, just before the curve, and we stopped, waited for them to move off. They stared at us, big-eyed and startled by our chorus of "*How does it feeeel, to be on your own, with no direction home...,*" and I wondered what they thought of us noisy humans, howling for no apparent reason.

They bounded off into the forest, and I told Dad he'd scared them, and Fred said, "No, it was you, Kit. You sound like a bullfrog," and just then the radio played Three Dog Night, belting out "*Jeremiah was a bullfrog...*" We all laughed like crazy, started singing along again, and drove on. The whole weekend was like that, totally free and easy, as if the chorus line "*Joy to the world*" got right inside us and kept us high. We did some fishing, ate when we felt like it, and one night we caught an amazing meteor shower. We swam, hiked and talked to the park ranger about the legend of Queneesh. He told us that's what the local First Nations folks call the Comox Glacier, and it means *great white whale.* I remember thinking that was sort of cool, was only half listening when he went on to talk about the perpetual snow on the mountains...

There's plenty of snow on the mountains now. I switch the radio to the oldies station but they aren't playing "Joy to the World." I don't recognize the tune at all, but I leave it and focus hard on following the narrow swathe of headlight beams on the road ahead.

fifTEEN

By the time we reach the Paradise Meadows parking lot in Strathcona Park, it's only 3:00 AM, still dark. The headlights flash over the sign for the trailhead to Forbidden Plateau, and I stop to point it out to Ike. "There's our route."

"Forbidden Plateau? We're going there?"

"It's the quickest access point." I park the car close by the sign and switch off the engine. We're plunged into deep, dark and absolute silence.

"Whooo," Ike says. "You know the old Native stories about Forbidden Plateau, don't you?"

I nod.

"Yeah? You know it's inhabited by evil spirits who eat women and children?"

I'm not going to let him get to me. "Good thing we aren't either one, eh?"

He snorts. "You're not a child?"

"Not. Listen, we've got one more thing to do before we go."

"What?"

"The video shot on the Blackberry. I didn't do it yet."

"Why doesn't that surprise me? Well, it's not like we can do it now, in the dark, can we?"

"The interior light in the car should be good enough. Remember that guy in the store told us the Blackberry can get video in low light?"

"Grainy and fuzzy video."

"That's good enough. I don't even know why we have to do a video anyway. What am I supposed to say?"

"*You* aren't supposed to say anything."

"What?"

"*I'm* going to do the talking. You got to write your stupid manifesto. I get to have my say on the video."

"Fine." And then the enormity of this pounds into me, breaking through a layer of icy detachment I didn't know I was wearing. "Ike, does this mean you've decided to stay with me? You're laying your life down too?"

"Yeah, man. Screw this life. I don't need it."

"But…it's not about that. It's about the mission."

He laughs. "If you say so. Come on, get the Blackberry and let's get this over with."

I want to argue with him, convince him this mission is noble, it's for the benefit of humanity and history, but another part of me whispers, No, don't talk him out of it. I don't want to do this alone. He can have his reasons, and I can have mine.

I rummage in the pack, find the Blackberry and then flip on the car's interior light. I study the Blackberry, being careful to keep my expression bland. I should have studied the manual so I'd know how to operate the video function. Only I didn't have a manual, did I? But if I tell Ike I need to figure it out, he'll get pissy, won't he?

"What's taking so long?"

I've got it now. I remember the guy at the store showing us how it works. I point the Blackberry at Ike and start filming. "Go."

Ike puts on this fake deep voice and says, "Good evening. Welcome to my world. So glad you could stop by. Heh heh. Kinda cool to be talking to you people of the future. If you're still here, that is. I'm not going to tell you about life now 'cause my bud here, Kit, he already did that and you'll probably have a good laugh reading his manifesto."

"Ike!" I hiss.

"Silence! No comments from the cheap seats." He lowers his voice and says, "That was Kit. Always causing trouble."

I grit my teeth and keep quiet.

"So, like I was saying. I'm going to give you a prediction. I'm predicting that if us lousy humans are still around, by now we look like aliens. You know, puny little bodies, gray skin and big fat heads with big round eyes. Ugly, man, real ugly."

"Ike!"

"Shut up, Kit. This is my bit. You want to know why I think they look like that? It's 'cause I don't believe in aliens. I think those little dudes some people see are *us*. Humans from the future who figured out how to time travel. It's us, coming back to see what people are supposed to look like. So take a good look, you little shits. You've probably trashed the planet, and you're living in holes in the ground so you've got that gray skin and big eyes like bugs or bats to see in the dark, and you've got machines hauling your skinny little asses around and doing all the work so your bodies are wasted. And you've got those huge ugly heads 'cause all you do is think, and you don't even screw each other 'cause you figured out how to live for five hundred years and you don't have room on the planet for any more babies. Am I right? You bet I'm right."

"Are you finished?" I whisper.

"Yeah, I'm finished."

I switch off the Blackberry. My hands are shaking. "Do you really believe what you just said?"

"Maybe. What's it to you?"

"Nothing," I say. "Nothing." It's useless to argue with him. I know he won't rethink this, won't want to send a kinder message to the future. That's Ike. Just who he is.

I tuck the Blackberry into my jacket pocket and lean back. "Let's rest a bit until it's light out, okay?"

"Whatever, man. Just as long as we don't screw up and sleep all day."

I turn off the light, turn the radio down low and close my eyes. I don't sleep. But in a way, I do leave myself. I imagine what this little scene would look like from space. There's me and Ike, slumped in the car. The car is the only vehicle in the parking lot.

I can see it, parked askew, the gravel space surrounding it, and around that are the trees. Fir, cedar, hemlock. I go higher and there are the mountains rising up; higher yet and I see the whole of Vancouver Island, then the continent of North America, the Pacific Ocean; Earth itself, a jewel, silver and blue, aloft in the black sea of space.

And way down there, a mere mote of insignificance, is me. Me with an *M*.

And then I hear Bob Marley, Marley with an *M*, singing, *"Don't worry, every little thing gonna be all right...,"* and I know he's trying to help me. An ember of peace glows in my chest, soft and warm, like a candle. Maybe it's not peace exactly. More like the absence of anxiety. I'm here. I'm finally doing what I said I'd do.

Behind my closed eyelids, there is light. I wait and the light strengthens and I know the dawn has come.

"Ike?"

"Yeah?"

"Let's go." We get out of the car, and the chill air makes me notice I need to pee, so I do that, right out in the open, leaving my mark in the snow. Then I pull on my gloves and my tuque, zip my jacket, get out the sled, load the computer and my pack, take hold of the rope. And start walking.

"You know the way?" Ike asks.

"Yeah."

"So which way is it?"

"Up."

"Up? That's it?"

"That's it."

It's beautiful on the mountain, a clear day dawning pink and gold, sharing its color with the snow, the sunlight glowing like halos from the frosted tips of the trees. Wow. Just, wow. This day was made for me. For my mission.

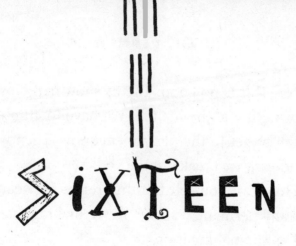

SIXTEEN

"How long we been walking now?" Ike asks.

"I don't know. Maybe a couple of hours. Maybe more."

"How much farther?"

"Come off it, Ike. You don't get to the top of a mountain in a couple of hours. It can take a couple of days."

"Dude, there's no way. We can't walk for a couple days. We'll be dead."

I can't help laughing. "Isn't that the whole idea?"

Ike laughs too. He laughs for so long I think maybe he's lost it. Finally, gasping, he asks, "So why not right here? This looks like a perfect spot. Let's break out the vodka."

"No. This is no good. There's snow here now, but by spring it'll all be melted. We have to climb high enough to get to the permanent snow. Then we dig in, and *then* we break out the vodka."

"How can you tell the difference between this snow and permanent snow? You're making that up."

"I'm not making it up."

"Yeah, you are. Snow is snow. All cold and white and too damn much of it, if you ask me."

"Ike, you're not getting cold feet are you?"

"Bad joke, man. Real bad."

"Sorry. Couldn't resist."

"Yeah, and I noticed you couldn't answer my question either. I'm telling you, this snow right here is fine."

"Ike, I've hiked here in the summer and there wasn't any snow on the ground. It only stays permanent way higher up, and if we don't go there, we're not going to be like Ötzi. We're just going to be a couple of stupid dead guys who get found in no time flat."

"That's good enough for me."

I can't believe he's saying this. After all his tough-guy talk, he's wimping out? I can understand him getting tired. I'm tired too, but not so much that I'm giving up. "It's *not* good enough for me."

"Of course not. Not for the perfect Kit. No. It has to be special. Gimme a break, man. This is it. I'm stopping."

"Fine. You stop. I'm going on."

"Go ahead. But give me the vodka."

"What? I'm not giving it to you. I'm going to need it."

"So who's the one who thought to bring it, huh? That was me. So I get it. Hand it over."

I stop. Now what? I have to convince him to go on, but how? I look around and notice a gap in the trees up ahead. "See that?"

"Yeah. So what?"

"So we go there, then we cut off the trail and go up a gully. I remember that spot. It's like a short cut. The climb will be a bit steeper, but we'll hit the perma snow way faster that way. Come on, Ike, you can do it, man."

"How long will it take?"

I shrug. "I can't say exactly. But I know that route to the peak cuts off a few hours."

He hesitates and finally says, "Okay. But you better not be lying or you're going to have one more thing in common with the Ice Man."

"What do you mean?"

"Forget it. Let's go."

We start walking again, but the pleasure I had in the hike has evaporated. I shouldn't have stopped. Somehow it's harder now to keep going. My legs feel about ten times heavier; just lifting them is an effort. The sled too has packed on weight. It's dragging behind me like a house. Or a noose. And that threat of Ike's...He wouldn't actually bash me on the head, would he? It's not like he has an arrow to shoot me with, but there are rocks around.

We keep going. I start to notice things I hadn't noticed before, like the numbness in my toes and the cold curling in around my neck. Maybe I was sweating and the halt was enough to let the sweat cool, and now the chill air seeks the moisture on my skin with probing tendrils. This air, it's thin. It's pure. It would be repulsed by sweat, wouldn't it? Its nature is to purify, to freeze all it finds, to transform it into dazzling shards of ice.

I love that purity. There, just to the side of the trail, I see flowers. The flowers are made of frost petals, intricately formed arrays of crystal. I'm reminded of my grandmother and her crystal collection. She showed me this book about it once. What I liked most about the book were the flowers that fluttered out from between the pages. She said, "Oh, I forgot I pressed these in here. They're from my favorite pansy."

I bend to examine the delicate furls, amazed at how some have nested in formations like the scales of a fish while others rise up in sparkling shards. When a sunbeam lights them, they take my breath away.

I shouldn't be taken in by the beauty. I know this. Beauty can betray. It can draw you close and then crumble in the instant you reach out to grasp it. It can leave you holding dust, with all the charm of dandruff.

I laugh aloud and call to Ike, "Dandruff."

He doesn't answer.

It takes longer than I thought it would to reach the gap in the trees, maybe because the snow is deeper now and it takes ever more effort to slog through it. Finally we make it, and I lead the way off the trail. Almost at once the going gets steeper, the snow we're trudging through deeper yet. We keep going, one step at a time, heads down, plodding. Then, suddenly, I'm in snow up to my chest, floundering, and far off I hear a roar.

Avalanche? No. It can't be. This isn't the place for it. The slope isn't steep enough. I've just stepped into a low spot, one hidden by the drifting snow. All I have to do is push on, forward, and I'll be clear. I draw a breath and it doesn't satisfy me. I need more air. Why? Not enough oxygen? Are we that high? If so, we must be getting close. I draw a few more breaths and it's no good, it's like sucking in dry ice. It hurts down deep, in my lungs. I close my mouth, notice my tongue feels thick. I force my feet to move. It's like pushing against a wall of clay, a substance almost set solid, one that gives up inches only grudgingly.

At last I'm clear of the dip, and I find myself jerking forward like a puppet on a string, expending far too much effort on the clear ground my feet have gained. I stagger to a halt, and in that moment a witching scream of wind slices the air. It cuts through me, right down to my marrow, past that, keeps cutting until it stabs, icicle sharp, into my soul.

It's the sound of nightmares. Of things not seen, only felt in the grim dark of our primitive past. It's the cry of cave lions, of wolves, of creatures with fangs and claws, on the hunt for warm blood. I go still, a creature of prey, aware only that I am weak, I've been found, and I am finished.

I wait, passive, and nothing happens. I'm not finished. We're in the open and the ice-salted wind is blasting down the face of the cliff that now confronts us.

"Holy shit," Ike says. "You think we're climbing that?"

I don't answer him. I'm still pulling back from the abyss. I don't remember the cliff being quite this daunting.

"We can't do this, dumbass! That's the sort of thing where you've gotta have special equipment. Ropes and axes and stuff. There's no way."

"Okay, okay," I gasp. "Let's just take a break and we'll figure it out. I'm sure there's a deer trail or something that cuts across the face. If we can find that..."

"A deer trail? A deer trail?" Ike guffaws, long and loud. "Give me the vodka, Kit."

"No. Not yet."

"I'm not going to drink it all. But I need a shot of courage if I'm going up a deer trail."

I look up at the cliff and decide maybe he's right; I'm desperately thirsty and a shot of courage might be something we both could use just now. I reach into my pack, find the vodka, unscrew the top, hand it to Ike. He takes a drink and hands it back. I take a drink. It burns like crazy going down my throat and hits my stomach like a punch. Then it spreads warmth, a slow burn, and I take another swig.

"Hey, not so fast," Ike says.

He takes another drink, and I take another, and then we sit down to study the cliff.

"You see the deer trail, Kit?"

"I'm looking."

"You sure this is the place?"

I hate to admit it, but I'm not sure. "Everything looks different in the winter."

"So you're not sure, are you? We're screwed, aren't we? Why the hell did I think, even for one lousy minute, that I could trust *you*, of all people, to get me to the top of a mountain?"

"You think you could do better?"

"Shit, man. The deer can do better."

I can't argue with that. I take another swallow of vodka and stare at the cliff. It's the final test, isn't it? The one we must pass in order to be worthy. I force myself to look methodically, moving my eyes in a careful grid pattern from side to side. And then I find it.

"Look. You see that?"

"What?"

I gesture with the vodka bottle, take a pull from it and gesture again. "Right there. That bluish rock sticking out on the left."

"I can't see it."

I get to my feet and for a slow, strange moment the planet tilts. What the hell? I stare at the vodka bottle in my hand and it's more than half empty. I blink, force my eyes to focus and point again. "There's a shrub there. On the left. See? And just above that, there's a rock."

Ike laughs. "So?"

I take a step forward. "Dammit!" I roar. "Open your eyes! It's right there! And if you look to the right of that, you can see a line."

"See a line."

"Ike. I'm trying to tell you, I found the trail. We can go."

"Forget it. Right here is fine."

Anger surges through me. I raise the vodka bottle and for one terrible second I'm tempted to smash it down on Ike's head. I can't do that. I drink instead and yell, "Right here is not fine. We have to go up!"

I start walking toward the cliff, and when I look down to check my footing, the snow is red. Blood red. The stain of red spreads around me, a jagged-edged spill of horror. I reel backward and fall. Someone died here! I can't catch my breath. I keep trying to draw in air, gulping it even, but it won't fill my lungs. I start crawling, scrabbling madly to free myself from this gruesome patch of hell, while my mind bucks and jigs, grappling for rationality.

I manage to choke out a single word. "Ike!"

He doesn't answer.

God. What have I done? Did I hit him? Did I? I dare a glance at the snow beneath me and it's white again, blessedly white, but I don't see Ike. I look toward the sled, where I left him, and someone else is standing beside it.

"Kit? Hey. It's me."

"You! You can't be here."

He nods. His voice is soft when he says, "I'm glad I am."

"Where's Ike? Do you see him?"

"What?"

"My friend, Ike! He was just here, and now...We have to find him!" I climb to my feet and stagger in a loopy circle, looking all around, not finding him, not finding him anywhere.

"Kit, buddy, you want to give that bottle to me?"

"What? Why?"

Why does he want it? What's he going to do? I gaze at the bottle and it's fine, still whole, no smears of red on the glass. But when I dare a look at the ground toward the cliff..."Do you see that?"

"See what?"

He can't see it?

"Kit? Come on. Let's go home."

I feel myself sway. I'm exhausted. Empty. Beaten. I sink down, into the snow. How did this happen? It shouldn't end like this. I point toward the blood and croak, "I don't know how that got there."

SEVENTEEN

The world is ice. I am immersed in it, a body frozen in a berg that rides a cold, black ocean. I can't move, can't blink, and know with absolute certainty that this is how it ends. There is no pain, not anymore, no will to command one last futile effort from my limbs. There is only ebbing consciousness, thoughts trickling into darkness. I watch them, not because I'm curious, but because they're all that's left.

My thoughts drift to my village, to my people. Did my companion make it back to them? Is he seated comfortably, warm before the fire? Do they sing from afar, chant the words of farewell to carry me safely beyond? I listen, and yes, there is a distant beat, a slow steady rhythm of soft thuds, inhalations and exhalations of breath. He should have taken the ax.

From across the void that separates us, I hear his voice now too. He's assuring me that all is well; he has come for me and will take me back. Take me back. Can it be possible? No, I must be dreaming. It is for me only, this task of...What is it I must do? I must go somewhere but the destination eludes me.

And then, at the base of the cliff, I see a magnificent white stag. For one long moment his dark liquid eyes hold mine, and then he tosses his head, gesturing sharply with his antlers. This way. He steps off with sure grace, and then he leaps, an astonishing float up onto the rock face.

He's here to guide me! I rise to my feet and follow. I feel like a thing of cement compared to him, a clumsy mass of foreign parts, but as I press on, I lighten. I set a foot into his hoofprint and it's as though he left a pool of energy there, a source of strength I can absorb through my soles. It flows into me and rises like the dawn, transmitting ripples of fur and wind, lightning, rock and alpine rivers. The force penetrates my veins, licks warm in my belly, snaps electric through my skin and into my hair. Joints are loosened, muscles strengthened, ligaments flexed.

My mind blazes and shimmers with a kaleidoscope of color, a vista of light streaming and expanding. I am young and green and strong. We climb, him leading, me following, and soon the sensation of effort leaves me. I can move with unbelievable ease, magical power. I have heard of this, the journey of the shaman, the flight between the worlds. Only once, in the manhood ritual, did I come close to this. It was a time of stinging pain when the indelible etching of black on skin marked me as one ready for the test, for my destiny. Is this stag my spirit totem? Where does he lead?

I hear music. The notes catch me, hold me. I mourn with the chanted lament. Go primal and pulsing with a drum. I shiver among rattles, slide high and low with voices rising and falling. When an electric guitar twangs in, I zing through a riff, until at last, dizzy and buzzing, I'm released on an echo.

It's difficult to find my bearings. The stag disappeared into the music, and I sense that something else is coming to take his place. I must wait. I sink into a small grove and rest in pale purple, enter dusky dreams of imagined things. I float on currents of juice, drift through meadows thick with scent, sip golden liquid and spiral into darkness.

Someone is speaking. Through a crack in my eyelids I see the ground moving past. It streams by steadily for a time, an expanse of white, and then there is a tiny pause, a jerk, and the ground moves again. At once I understand. My companion has laid me on a travois for the journey back to our village. My eyes fall shut and I wonder again if I am dreaming. I was so certain of death, so ready to accept my fate. A flash of light cuts across my eyes, cuts through a swathe of thick curtain, and there, on the other side, I glimpse Fred.

I call out to him. "Hey! Over here." He turns and looks at me. I see his mouth move, forming words, but I can't hear them. And then the curtain falls back and he's gone. It seems to me he wanted something. What? Was I supposed to get something?

Yes. I was to have gathered blackberries. I didn't want to be reduced to the company of those who pluck berries. Such tasks fall only to the weak, to the damaged who cannot trek forth on the hunt. I was among the warriors once, a fearless participant in the tests of skill. I ran with the youth, wrested victory from my opponents, was admired by the women. The only remnant of that time now covers my head, the skin of a bear I once took when I was strong, when I was a man of courage and honor.

Is it too late for that now? Can I find what I must for Fred? For all the world, past and present? Future? I am apart from it now, isolated from them all. I hear their voices surrounding me, their whispers and murmurs rising and falling. They move in the light, pure and dazzling, and they are everywhere, part of everything. They bear messages and they are singing a song of oneness, of gossamer threads touching, joining each particle of the universe. They sing of layers, of finding the web spun like gold from eye to heart to hand, and none are separate, none overlooked. Each leaf, each child, deer, blade of grass, ocean, mountain, prisoner, puppy, breeze, monk— all are one.

Except for me. I am a ghost in their midst, suspended between the worlds. I need to know one last thing. I ask, "Am I dead?"

And a voice says, "You should rest now."

EighTEEN

"Fred?"

"Hey, bud. How're you doing?"

I try looking around, but it's no good. The light hurts. "Where are we?"

"We're in the hospital. The doctor says you've got to stay here for a bit. Mom and Dad are here too, but they've just been called away to talk to a… specialist."

It's like wading through sludge, making my brain comprehend this. "Why are we in the hospital?"

"You've got first-stage hypothermia. Not to mention you had a damn scary blood-alcohol count. Close to toxic."

Alcohol? The sludge thins and I find a word lurking. Vodka. And blood. Yes, those two go together. But how? Blood, vodka.

Oh, God.

I lift my head and shoulders from the bed and look around, but all I can see are white curtains. "Where's Ike?"

"Easy, buddy. You're not supposed to get up yet. Who's Ike?"

"Ike! My friend, Ike. Where is he?"

Fred looks away. "I don't know, man. You want me to call him for you?"

Call him? Call him? I slump back. He means on the phone.

"I don't have his number."

"Oh."

The sludge shifts, swirls, and this time I bolt fully upright. Bad move, because everything moves, and not the way it's supposed to.

"Kit! Would you just take it easy?" Fred puts a hand on my chest and pushes until I'm lying back again. He yanks the blankets over me and growls, "Stay."

I stare up at him, but my gut is making some funky moves and I can't speak. I breathe and my gut sort of settles into gurgling, and I say, "How did we get here?"

"I figured out where you went from a map you left on your desk. I tracked you, we met up and then you passed out. So I brought you down the trail on the sled, put you in my car and, shazam, here we are."

"But didn't Ike come too? You saw him, right?"

He shakes his head. "No, man. It was just you."

"God," I moan. And the moan grows, rising and swelling, not as sound but as molten horror and guilt. I bite down on the pillow, dig my fingers into the bed, but tears and snot spew out of me. My entire body convulses.

"Oh, man! Little bro." And Fred gets right beside me and wraps his arms tight around me, but it keeps heaving out, rolling and falling in hot, fat blobs.

I don't recognize the voice that eventually speaks, but somehow I know it's me whispering, "I killed him. I killed him."

And Fred, I know his voice, he says, "No, Kit. Nobody got killed. There was just you, no one else, no other tracks. It was *just you* up there."

He's lying. I stiffen, go still, and he eases back.

Someone, a nurse or whatever, sticks her head through the opening in the curtains and says, "Is everything okay, here?"

Fred shakes his head. "I don't know. I guess he's upset. Can you do something for him?"

She eyeballs me and says, "I'm sorry. The doctor on duty has requested a psych exam, and we'd rather not give any meds until after that happens." She purses her lips and adds, "His system needs to flush out the alcohol first anyway."

She withdraws.

I look at Fred. "You don't need to cover for me."

"What're you talking about?"

"You don't. They'll find out sooner or later. And then you'll be in trouble too. And I deserve whatever..."

"I'm not covering for you. I swear to God, you were alone up there."

"Yeah? What about the blood in the snow? What about that?"

He frowns. "Blood?" And then his face clears and he actually grins. "You mean the algae bloom? Pretty weird, eh?"

"What?"

"You know, I'd heard about it, but that was the first time I'd seen it. There's a certain type of algae that grows in snow in late winter or early spring and looks like blood."

Again with the sludge, bogging down my brain. "Are you making that up?"

"Nope. I can prove it to you, soon as we're home. It's in one of my geography texts."

I don't think he's lying. And the rush of relief makes me limp. "Wow."

Fred nods.

"So you saw the red snow?"

He nods again.

"But you're saying you didn't see anyone else or any other tracks?"

Another nod.

"Yeah? Well, I can prove something too."

"What's that?"

"Where's my jacket?"

He rolls his eyes. "We're not leaving."

"I just need to get something out of the pocket. Where is it?"

In reply, Fred stretches his arm over to the chair near the foot of the bed and holds my jacket aloft. "Which pocket?"

"The one on the inside. On the right, I think."

He feels around in the pocket; his eyebrows rise when his hand closes around something and out comes the Blackberry. He whistles. "Nice. When did you get this baby?"

I feel heat in my face as I shake my head and reach for it. He places it in my palm and leans back, waiting. My hands tremble as my fingers try to locate the right buttons, but finally I get it figured out and tilt the small screen on the Blackberry toward Fred.

"Now watch. I'll show you Ike."

I select *Play* and a grainy image appears.

"What's that?" Fred asks.

"It's a video of the passenger seat in Mom's car. See, there's the side window. And there's Ike's burger wrapper. And…"

Something's wrong. Where's Ike?

"Didn't you say I'd see Ike?" Fred asks.

"Yes. Shh. It'll start any second now."

We wait in silence, and then a voice on the video says, "*Ike!*"

A few seconds later, we hear that again. "*Ike!*" More time ticks by and then there's "*Are you finished?*"

And that's all.

The horror I felt only minutes before pales beside what I feel now. I yank the Blackberry onto my chest and stare at it.

"Kit?"

"Wrong it something with."

"Huh? You want to try that one again?"

"I again, yeah, try."

"Kit, you're mixing up…Never mind. Anyway, it seems like the sound worked okay. Maybe you should just rest."

"No. Work didn't. Just minute, wait. Fix it I have to."

Fred stays quiet and I focus fiercely on how to replay the video. There used to be a rewind for everything. "Rewind everything," I mutter.

"Okay," says Fred.

The Blackberry emits a tiny chime and it should be ready, but now I can't operate my fingers. "Bullshit, what!"

Fred holds out a hand. "You want me to try, bud?"

I drop the poisonous thing on the bed, and Fred picks it up. He says, "Okay. Looks fairly straightforward. You've got it set to play, right?"

I jerk a nod in his direction.

"Right. So have you got hours of video on here or what? Is the Ike shot near the beginning or the end?"

"Know don't."

He sighs. "No problem. I'll just keep watching until I find it." He selects *Play* and keeps his eyes glued to the screen. I keep my eyes glued to him.

But just a couple of minutes later, Fred shrugs. "It's just got that same bit again, with the car seat and you saying 'Ike' a couple of times and..."

"Do videos of dead people disappear?"

"Say what?"

"If you die, are you erased?"

Fred blinks. "No, man. We've seen videos of old Aunt Annie, and our dog Harry, right? They didn't disappear. And there are plenty of movies out there starring dead actors."

"It's impossible."

He frowns, opens his mouth, looks like he does when he's going to argue. But then he just slumps back and looks at the floor.

"Fred?"

"Yeah?"

"Ike was on that video. I was there with him and I filmed it."

He nods. Then his face flushes deep red and his hand clenches, forms a fist that he uses to tap against his mouth. After a moment, the fist falls to the bed and he whispers, "Have I ever lied to you, Kit? Have I? Am I a liar?"

"What the hell?"

"'Cause I'm going to tell you something. And it's the truth. And it's this. *There is no Ike*! He's not real. Can you get that, please? He's just some sort of imaginary friend you've got, like some little kid thing in your head. Okay? *There's no Ike.*"

My lips feel numb, but I make them move anyway. "Why are you saying this?"

His fist uncurls and his hand lies there, palm up. His blue eyes shimmer with unshed tears and he croaks, "'Cause I love you, man. And I can't stand seeing you like this anymore."

And then the curtain slides back, and there's Mom and Dad and this little woman wearing glasses who says, "Hello, Kit. I'm Dr. Hayes. I'm a psychiatrist and I'd like to chat with you for a bit."

But I don't hear what she says next because I'm watching Fred give the Blackberry to Dad, watching as he mutters something, watching as he leaves.

He simply disappears beyond that curtain, and then, about two seconds later, there's Ike saying, "Hey."

I yell, "Fred! Come back. Ike's here!"

Dr. Hayes says, "Who is here, Kit?"

Ike chuckles. "Looks like you blew it, dumbass."

I close my eyes and nod. "Yeah. Guess I did."

I hear my mother crying, my father murmuring softly and Dr. Hayes saying, "There are ways we can help."

"Will you help me get up the mountain?" I ask.

"I'll try." She sits on the chair by the bed and says, "Can you tell me about it?"

author's note

The main character in this story, Kit Latimer, experiences the onset of a mental-health disorder that falls under the umbrella of an illness known as schizophrenia. It is estimated that as much as one percent of our population suffers from schizophrenia, and it's not an illness that is normally ever considered wholly cured. However, if the illness is detected and treated in the early stages, the outcome can be very good— good enough to allow the sufferer to lead a relatively normal life.

The symptoms of schizophrenia vary from person to person, and since no definitive tests are as yet available, diagnosis of the illness is made by qualified professionals based on particular behaviors. For males, symptoms generally begin to occur between their mid-teen years and early twenties, and for females, from the mid-twenties to around the age of thirty. This is only a generalization because schizophrenia can occur in children and, even more rarely, in the elderly. Comprehensive lists of the more common symptoms of the illness are available from numerous sources, including the Internet. One site with a list of symptoms can be found at http://www.schizophrenia.com/. A site with information especially for youth is http://www.psychosissucks.ca/epi/.

Some of the symptoms generally referred to as "negative" include lethargy, low interest in social or other formerly enjoyed activities, difficulty with speech or physical coordination, and lack of emotions. "Positive" symptoms, including hallucinations and delusions, feel entirely real to those experiencing them. One of the most common hallucinations is hearing voices, and very often these voices are abusive.

If the afflicted person also suffers from paranoia, their suspicions and distrust may be directed toward those who are close to them, and in many cases they don't recognize that anything is wrong. For these reasons, it can be difficult to convince the sufferer to see a doctor. Other trusted people, such as family, friends or school counselors, should be enlisted to help, and the sooner help is found, the more likely it is that treatment will be effective.

As I researched schizophrenia and worked through the creation of this story, I developed an ever deeper sympathy for those with mental illness.

It was often emotionally exhausting for me to continue imagining what my character was experiencing, and if it is hard to imagine, I believe it must be incredibly stressful and harsh to live with. It is my hope that we all come to a greater understanding of mental illnesses and do our utmost as individuals and as a society to treat the afflicted among us with compassion.

K.L. Denman

acknowledgments

This book could not have been written without the support of some dear friends and family. My husband, Ron Denman, often lent a patient ear and encouraged me to persevere when I voiced doubts. I am grateful to Dr. Peter Uhlmann, psychiatrist, for generously taking time to read and provide valuable comments on an early draft. I also wish to thank Lin Johnson, former director of the Powell River Schizophrenic Society, for reading a later version of this story and for introducing me to a wonderful young man and his mother who were willing to speak to me about their experiences with psychosis. I owe thanks to Andrew Wooldridge, publisher at Orca, for believing that *Me, Myself and Ike* had the potential to become a novel. Finally, I deeply appreciate the work of Sarah Harvey, my editor at Orca; her professional expertise, insightful commentary and cheerful approach were vital to completing this story.

K.L. Denman was born in Calgary, Alberta, and spent her childhood in a house one street away from the open prairie. When she was eleven, her family moved to Delta, British Columbia, and she got to know life on the coast. Today she lives on a small farm on British Columbia's Sunshine Coast with her family of people, two dogs, three cats, two horses and an elderly mule. More information about Kim is available on her blog at http://kldenman.blogspot.com/.